# "Maybe you could come and be our new mommy," Gina said, tilting her head.

Matt cringed. "Quiet, kitten. You can't ask a stranger to be your mommy. I'm sorry," he said to Justine as his five-year-old daughter ran off to play. "I didn't see that one coming at all."

"Relax. I'm fairly positive you didn't recruit her as a matchmaker," Justine assured him. Then a teasing light entered her eyes. "So has Gina recruited any other good possibilities?"

"I think maybe she just did," he quipped, then nearly swallowed his tongue. Where had that come from? He'd just flirted with the new minister.

He just couldn't seem to think of her as Reverend Clemens. Since the moment he'd set his eyes on her, she'd been a beautiful woman he'd really wanted to meet and get to know. How to do that with a minister, however, would take a little thought.

## Books by Kate Welsh

### KATE WELSH

is a two-time winner of Romance Writers of America's coveted Golden Heart Award and a finalist for RWA's RITA® Award in 1999. Kate lives in Havertown, PA, with her husband of over thirty years. Kate has a married daughter. And with the marriage came a wonderful new son. Her happy home includes one remaining daughter, a Chespeake Bay retriever and a cat he wishes would be his friend.

There are few crafts Kate hasn't tried. Those ideas she can't resist grace her home and those of her friends and family. But she refuses to discuss her addiction to do-it-yourself TV and all those lovely projects waiting on the back burner!

As a child she often lost herself in creating make-believe worlds and happily-ever-after tales. Kate turned back to creating happy endings when her husband challenged her to write down the stories in her head. With Jesus so much a part of her life, Kate found it natural to incorporate Him into her writing. Her goal is to entertain her readers with wholesome stories of the love between two people the Lord has brought together and to teach His truth while she entertains.

# HOME TO
# SAFE HARBOR

## KATE WELSH

Published by Steeple Hill Books™

Special thanks and acknowledgment
are given to Kate Welsh for her contribution
to the SAFE HARBOR series.

STEEPLE HILL BOOKS

Steeple
Hill™

ISBN 0-373-87220-8

HOME TO SAFE HARBOR

Visit us at www.steeplehill.com

**Printed in U.S.A.**

I am the light of the world. He who follows Me
shall not walk in darkness, but have the light of life.
—*John* 8:12

For Miranda and Erica—
Nothing is so precious as good health or the beauty
that shines from within you, because God is within
you. He will always see your beauty as long as you
love Him. Keep up the good work. We all love you
and are proud of you for how far you've come.

# Chapter One

Reverend Justine Clemens stood frozen before the entire congregation of First Peninsula Church, managing to hold a smile in place through sheer determination. In her hands, she held the plaque she'd just accepted amid thunderous applause. Clearly, everyone thought she should be thrilled.

They were certainly thrilled.

But she was devastated.

The sign on her new office door would not read "Reverend Justine Clemens—Assistant Pastor." That's what she'd thought Reverend Burns and the board meant when they'd asked her to stay on permanently to assist him. Instead the plaque she now held tightly clutched in her hands read "Reverend Justine Clemens—Women and Youth Pastor."

Once again she'd been relegated to a traditional

role for women in the church. Once again she was on the road to having no one and nothing to call her own.

When Reverend Burns retired—and at seventy, how far off could that be?—she'd thought these people would be her flock. That they would look to her for guidance. Be her family. How could she have so completely misunderstood this position? Had it been wishful thinking? Self delusion?

The corners of the brass plaque bit into her hands and she managed to relax her trembling grip just a little. But, as she did, she also had to blink back the tears that threatened to give her away. Reverend Burns had just handed her what he clearly thought of as first prize, but she knew it to be the honorable mention it was.

He stood next to her at the front of the church, smiling and looking more like a man of sixty these days. When she'd visited him following his first knee surgery last March he'd looked all of his seventy years plus a few.

"There's been a lot of speculation that I'm ready for long days fishing or even quieter days reading my worn and ragged Bible," Reverend Thomas Burns told his congregation, that precious book held lovingly in his hand. "Well, I'm here to tell you I've never felt younger." He smiled fondly down from the top step of the altar and used his other hand to pat his rapidly thinning girth. "It's a miracle what new knees and exercise will do for a body.'' He chuckled. ''Mine, anyway.''

At a sudden clearing of Dr. Robert Maguire's throat, scattered chuckles echoed through the sanctuary. Reverend Burns blushed a bit. ''I know. I know,'' he said pointing at the doctor. ''You've been telling me this for years. And you were right. To be honest with all of you, I had considered retiring. During my enforced downtime, though, I found out rather quickly that I'd go loopy if I did. And I don't think the Lord would be happy with a man in his prime hanging up his robes.'' Reverend Burns moved closer to Justine, placing his hand on her shoulder. ''Well, now, enough about me. Back to the reason I asked the board to hire Reverend Clemens in this new capacity. For a long time I've been feeling out of touch with some of you. So when I noticed how well Justine was able to relate to the younger women and teens, it seemed best for everyone to bring her on board permanently as pastor to the women and youth of First Peninsula Church.

''I also want to thank you all for making my young friend feel welcome and for proving Thomas Wolfe wrong. You really can go home again, and we're all glad she's come back to us. The ladies of the Safe Harbor Women's League have put together a little luncheon to officially welcome Reverend Clemens. Won't you join us in the church hall?''

Justine blindly followed Reverend Burns out of the sanctuary and down the steps that led to the first-floor basement and the church hall. The morning light streamed through the high arched windows and fell on the mural the church's administrative assistant, Kit Peters, had recently done on the side wall. Justine felt a little peace descend on her troubled soul as she gazed at the pastoral scene of trees and rolling hills and the distant flock of sheep tended by a gentle-eyed Jesus.

There was a lot of activity and laughter in the kitchen at the far end of the room, where an array of beverages was already set out on the stainless-steel counter between the hall and kitchen. Folding tables and chairs were scattered around the highly polished hardwood floor. A giant banner stretched above the kitchen pass-through read *Welcome Home to Safe Harbor.*

Of course, she'd been back in Safe Harbor for six months. She'd returned to her hometown for the first time in ten years to answer a call for help from Reverend Burns—a call that couldn't have come at a better time. The day before he'd contacted her asking her to fill in for him, she'd gotten upsetting news. The inner-city Chicago church where she'd served since divinity school had decided to hire a much younger and less experienced minister—a man—to replace the retiring pastor. What had distressed her the most was that the recommendation had come from the pastor to whom she'd been an assistant for ten years.

She had been hurt and seeking God's guidance when Reverend Burns called asking for her help. She'd talked to him earlier in the week and he'd mentioned the possibility of needing surgery, but then he'd fallen while trying to help in the search for one of Holly Douglas's five-year-old twin boys. Little Aidan had gotten lost on the nature trails in a sudden early-March snowstorm. Aidan was found, and the accident had seemed an answer to prayers, for Justine as well as for Reverend Burns. It had given her the chance to gain perspective and to rediscover the peace and love of her hometown.

She loved Reverend Burns like a father. Certainly more than she did her own faithless father. The reverend had led her to the Lord in her rebellious youth, and his kindly guidance had influenced her to pursue a vocation in ministry. But now, standing at what was supposed to be a celebration of her new position, Justine felt only hurt and disappointed by her mentor and friend. Following his lead, she took off her robe and hung it in the closet, still hiding her inner turmoil.

*What are you telling me, Lord?*

The hall filled quickly and everyone was in the mood to celebrate. Everyone but Justine. She somehow managed to keep a bright face on, as one after another, members of the congregation stopped to congratulate her on her new position.

"You're upset," Reverend Burns said when he returned to her side about half an hour later with coffee for them. His brows were drawn together in a worried frown.

Justine started and felt a blush heat her face. If he knew, did everyone know?

"Relax. I doubt anyone else noticed, but I know you too well to be fooled by that pasted-on smile. What is it, dear?"

Justine had never been able to hide the truth from Reverend Burns, not from that first day he'd caught her cutting school and enjoying a cigarette behind the gazebo in Safe Harbor Park with her new friends.

"I thought you asked me to stay on to be your assistant."

Reverend Burns's eyebrows climbed, further laddering his lined forehead. "That's exactly what you will be."

Justine turned the plaque she still held toward him. "But it's a ministry limited to women and children."

The older man sighed, shaking his head slightly. "You're still seeing the glass half-empty, Justine. You are an absolute wonder with the teens and younger women, not to mention the little ones. You relate to them in a way I find I no longer can. They make up a good portion of the congregation.

I want them going to you for help. You can do a lot of good.''

She was embarrassed by what sounded like selfish motives. "I feel as if it's happening again." The words tumbled out. "I thought I was being put in position to take your place one day. And I know you and the board wouldn't have limited the scope of my ministry if you had confidence in me that I could replace you. It feels like Chicago all over again."

"But it isn't the same, and we do have confidence in you," Reverend Burns said gently. "Don't let the human failings of some of God's servants take your eyes and trust off Him. And seek His plan for your life, dear, not your own. I very much fear that is what you've been doing all along." He held up his hand to stop her automatic defense. "I'm not saying your call to the ministry wasn't real. I'm saying that maybe He has something for you that you're blind to. I don't know what His plan is, but for now, why not do the job He's sent you and see what comes of it?"

Justine nodded jerkily, trying to hold back the emotions that surged in her. She could see the wisdom in his words, but following his advice would be a challenge.

"Excuse me, Reverend Clemens. Reverend Burns." A deep voice interrupted her struggle for composure. "I wonder if I might have a word with you before the kids descend on us."

Past hurts and new ones flew out of Justine's mind when she followed the sound of that husky voice to a point just over her head.

It was *him*.

At five foot ten, she wasn't used to looking up at many people. At least, not as far as she had to look up right now. She found herself snared by eyes an even deeper brown than her own. They were nearly obsidian.

For weeks she'd seen Matthew Trent around town and in church, and now she had a voice to put with that hauntingly handsome face. A dangerous combination of tall, dark and gorgeous, he was the new chief of police, and he distracted Justine every time she noticed him. Once, even in the middle of a sermon!

No man had ever affected her the way he did. No man had ever taken her eyes off her ministry, or made her heart pump harder with the simple sound of his voice. She watched as Reverend Burns turned to him with a friendly smile.

"Chief Trent, what can we do for you?"

"Actually, I wondered if one or both of you might be able to give me a little advice regarding a sixteen-year-old and trouble."

Reverend Burns held up his hand. "No time like the present to bow to the younger generation. I'll leave you to Justine's wisdom. There's a reason we hired her and this is it."

"But you know I still rely on your guidance,"

she protested, slightly alarmed at the thought of being alone with Matthew Trent. Justine took a fortifying breath, trying to still her pounding heart. What was wrong with her? They were in a room with more than a hundred people. Instead of protesting further, she forced a smile and nodded toward some empty tables in the far corner of the reception room.

"Would you mind sitting, Chief Trent?" she asked, hoping that with a table between her and the former FBI agent she would feel less distracted and intimidated by him. Calm and cool, he clearly didn't experience any of the terrifying feelings in her presence that she felt in his.

"Please. Make it Matt," he said, and moved toward the nearest empty table.

She was tempted not to respond in kind, wanting the distance her ministerial title gave her, but she knew that wouldn't be right. Trying to ignore Matthew Trent's blatant masculinity, Justine followed him to the table he'd chosen.

"Is this okay, Reverend Clemens?" He pulled out a chair for her at a table away from the others. "I don't want anyone to overhear and guess who we're talking about."

She smiled at that. Did he really think she didn't already know who the misdirected teen was? "Call me Justine and tell me what Alan Tobridge has done now."

He grimaced. "Am I that obvious?"

"No. But Alan is." Justine grinned. "Unfortunately, I can relate to exactly what he's going through. You haven't been here very long, but you'll eventually hear about my own rebellious years."

Matt chuckled. "What did you do? Cover your bible in bright purple? Wear red to church?"

Justine tried to ignore the tingle the low timber of his quiet laughter chased along her spine. "No," she said, distracted and strangely drawn to this man who was so concerned for someone else's child. "But I do remember having red and purple liberty spikes once upon a time."

"Liberty spikes?"

She grinned, suddenly relishing the opportunity to burst his stereotype bubble, though she usually cringed at talk of her turbulent youth. "First you take white glue, then you grab sections of hair…" She pulled a piece of hair straight out to the side to illustrate. Grinning, she tilted her head, leaving a long silence.

He broke it with a groan. "How could you say something like that to a man raising three daughters all by himself? I mean, you're a minister. If you pulled stunts like that, I'm doomed."

She'd observed him with his daughters. It was easy to see the love and affection within his family. "Sorry, I just couldn't resist. What I'm getting at is, I think Alan and I have a few things in common. My mother forgot I was alive most of the time."

Justine let her gaze survey the party before making eye contact with Matthew Trent. "Arlene and Jeffrey Tobridge aren't bad people, but they've bought heavily into relative morality. They let Alan do whatever he wants. If it feels good, it's okay. When he makes bad choices, they go to bat for him to get him out of trouble. My kid, right or wrong."

Matthew nodded. "I don't think he's a bad kid. I think he's trying to get their attention and their love. When they came to the station last night to pick him up, you could almost see the kid begging them to say they couldn't condone his behavior. But they have every intention of having the flower beds he destroyed up at the Lighthouse B & B replaced professionally. They've also offered to pay for the bracelet he walked off with from The Quest last week. Plus they've already arranged to have the library cleaned after he let that skunk loose in there."

Matt sighed and ran a hand through his short hair. "I know Judge Howard is going to go along with more parental restitution. And it isn't going to stop the way Alan's acting out. Charles Creasy held the parents responsible when he had my job and the judge always agreed with him. In a way they are, but— I don't even know why I'm bothering you about this." He frowned looking troubled. "Yes, I do. Do you have any idea how I stop this kid? Somebody's going to get hurt and he's going to ruin his life trying to prove his parents really do love him. What got you out of liberty spikes?''

Justine's eyes were on the senior pastor as he chatted with an engaged couple, and she smiled. ''Reverend Burns talked me out of my spikes and into the church. He convinced me I was only hurting myself—and I was. Nobody suffered but me if I skipped school, or dyed my hair some outrageous color, or smoked or stayed out all night. As I said, my mother barely knew I was around. But Alan is hurting others in trying to get his parents to put the brakes on his antics. I tried stopping him on the street after the library incident, but it was no go.'' She leaned forward. ''So I have another idea. Unfortunately, you'd have to supervise him, and I'd need to get Russ and Annie Mitchard to agree. After all, he hurt them when he stole the bracelet from Russ's shop and destroyed Annie's beautiful flower beds. I think Alan needs to see how his actions affect his victims by working off his debts to them.'' She relaxed against the back of her chair. ''The Mitchards' feelings need to be taken into account, though. They may not want to deal with him.''

Matthew Trent's eyes widened and he nodded. ''What an insightful idea. I have no problem supervising the kid, but who's going to talk Judge Howard into this?''

Justine pointed toward Reverend Burns and said

conspiratorially. "The judge's godfather, our pastor."

Matthew's mouth kicked up on one side in an endearing grin, just as all the children thundered into the hall with their teachers. "Daddy," a cherub-cheeked five-year-old girl shouted and ran to Matthew. Her cap of curly chestnut-brown hair and dark eyes mirrored those of her adoring father.

"Hi, kitten," he said, standing and swinging the little girl up high into his arms.

Justine found it hard to look at them together. There were times she wished she had the courage to take a chance on love and a family, but those things were not for her. She couldn't be a pastor *and* a mother. Leading a church was too demanding. It wouldn't be fair to the children. And besides that, she couldn't be a mother without first being a wife, and she'd never trust any man with her heart. She'd watched firsthand what could happen to a woman who loved and lost. Especially when the man appeared to be all that was brave, heroic and trustworthy. It only hurt more to be betrayed by the likes of a George Clemens. Or a Matthew Trent.

# *Chapter Two*

Matt had never been so relieved to see his kids. What had begun as a sort of strategy session with the new youth pastor had become uncomfortably… well… comfortable.

Originally he'd considered waiting till Reverend Burns was alone, but he'd foolishly disdained the cowardly impulse.

So what if he'd noticed Justine Clemens's golden hair flying in a brisk wind off the lake the very day he'd first set foot in this little town to interview with the mayor and town council. So what if, for the first time in well over two years, he'd felt the sharp sting of desire for a woman. And so what if he'd been thoroughly embarrassed to learn the woman who'd reawakened that part of his life was the new minister at First Peninsula Church.

Like an idiot he'd tempted fate and approached both ministers to seek advice. And seconds later, instead of talking with two ministers or the older man, Matt had found himself talking with a bright and friendly woman named Justine. A woman he'd already known he was very attracted to. She'd turned out to be not just beautiful, but kind and funny and wise, as well.

"Girls, say hello to Reverend Clemens," he told the three children, as he held his youngest daughter in his arms.

"Hello, Reverend," the older two girls said in unison.

Gina, his five year old imp, really did have all the curiosity of a kitten. She tilted her head, scrunched her face and obediently said, "Hi." Then, in his ear and in a kind of wet stage whisper, she continued, "She's a lady and she don't look at all like Reverend Burns."

Justine blinked, then laughed, clearly having heard. "All ministers aren't men and we don't all look like Reverend Burns."

Gina stared at Justine for a moment. "Do you got a husband?" she asked, her curiosity obviously caught by the idea of a female minister.

"No," Justine answered, matching Gina's serious tone perfectly.

Gina's frown deepened. "Maybe you could

come be our new mommy. Daddy'd share us. He's pretty used to it 'cause he had to share us with our sick dead mommy.''

Matt cringed and wanted to crawl under the table. "Quiet, kitten, you can't ask a stranger to be your mother. Remember, we talked about this already. I'm sorry," he said to Justine. "I didn't see that one coming at all.''

Wagging her stubby little finger to emphasize each word, Gina explained patiently, "But, Daddy, you got to listen. You said I can't ask an already married lady to be our mommy. I asked this time. See I 'membered what you told me after I asked Ms. Dalton back at my old school to come live with us.''

Matt's heartbeat sped up at the sound of Justine's chuckle. Flustered, he all but begged his oldest daughter, "Leslie, would you take the girls over and get them a little snack? We'll talk about this later, kitten.''

At thirteen, Les was such a big help. She had become a regular little mother to her nine- and five-year-old sisters. He didn't know what he'd do without her. With a little nod of her head and a little roll of her eyes, Les ushered Cindy and Gina toward the kitchen.

"Relax, I'm fairly positive you didn't recruit her as a matchmaker," Justine assured him.

"Count on it! Last spring she noticed all the kids in her preschool had mommies. She started a campaign to get one for herself. My late wife, Diane, once told me that as soon as your children can talk, you no longer have the luxury of pride. She's forever being proven right by Gina."

Justine chuckled again—and again his heart rolled in his chest.

"She's adorable. Don't give it another thought." Then a teasing little light entered Justine's brown eyes. "So how come you and this Ms. Dalton aren't an item."

"That was back in Green Bay." He sighed. "I honestly thought the campaign was over. And *Mrs.* Dalton wasn't exactly my type. She was an assistant teacher at Gina's preschool. I'm afraid Mr. Dalton, who had been married to Mrs. Dalton for nearly fifty years, would have been just a little upset to lose her to a younger man."

"I imagine he would. Has Gina recruited any other good possibilities?"

"I think maybe she just did," he quipped, then nearly swallowed his tongue. Where had that come from? He'd just flirted with the new minister!

Justine blushed and turned away, gesturing across the room. "I see Russ and Annie Mitchard over by the mural. I think we should ask them how our little plan to straighten out Alan sits with them. You'll have to let me know how it all works out in the end, if they agree."

As they approached Russ and Annie, Matt was sorry Justine had cut the conversation off, but at the same time, he was grateful. He just couldn't seem to go back to thinking of her as Reverend Clemens. Then again, he never really had. Since the moment he had first set his eyes on her, she'd been a beautiful woman he really wanted to meet and get to know. Deciding how to do that with a minister, however, would take a little thought.

Three days later Judge Howard sentenced Alan Tobridge to two hundred hours of community service. For the next several months he'd be Matt's responsibility three afternoons a week and every other Saturday. Judge Howard also levied a fine of five hundred dollars to help defray the cost of Alan's vandalism up at Annie Mitchard's B & B. The teen wouldn't have much time to get in trouble because he had to work off the fine with a part-time job at The Quest. Matt had stopped to tell Russ at the silversmith's shop first, and then he'd gone to tell Russ's wife Annie, up at the B & B.

Now, on his way back down Lake Drive, he noticed Justine walking across the street toward Market Square. He imagined she was on her way to the church to get ready for Wednesday evening services. It seemed only neighborly to stop and tell her how court had gone and to offer her a ride.

Matt gave a short *bleep* on his siren to get her attention as he coasted to a stop behind her. She glanced over her shoulder, then walked back to his squad car as he lowered the window. He could tell her smile was automatic because she seemed to catch herself, straighten and put on an expression he guessed she thought made her look ministerial. He grinned. To him she just looked kind of cute trying not to look like a knockout.

"Was I about to jaywalk or something, Chief Trent?"

"I thought we'd established that I'm Matt. And no, you're still on the right side of the law. I wanted to let you know how Alan's hearing went this afternoon."

"Oh?"

"Reverend Burns must have done a good sales job."

"Then, the judge went along?"

"Howard went with the whole plan. Want a lift? I could probably be going your way, and I can let you know the specifics."

She looked as if she might accept but then shook her head. "The exercise is good for me, and this weather won't last long now that summer's almost over."

Matt couldn't argue with that, even though he wanted to, so he nodded, bid her a good day and drove on. He wished he could get her out of his head, because, after two gentle rebuffs, he'd begun to think she didn't want to be there.

Maybe she wasn't ready to explore a relationship. When Justine had first gotten his attention, he'd felt disloyal to Diane. Then he'd remembered how Diane, a few days before her death, had made him promise not to cry, not to grieve too long and not to stay alone too long. She'd been right. Even with the girls, he was lonely. They were the center of his world—his link to the woman he'd chosen as his life partner. But they weren't enough.

Little by little his life had filled in. He'd had a good career with the FBI. It was interesting and challenging. But when Cindy was nearly kidnapped, he'd made his first big decision for the girls' welfare on his own. Before that, missing Diane's sensitive and insightful opinions, he'd turned to his in-laws for advice.

That had backfired, of course.

Mary and Seth Gainer had been like parents to him, but slowly he'd noticed their becoming intrusive. He had lost count of the times he'd come home from work to find they had arrived uninvited and sent the girls' sitter home for the day. Or the times he'd planned an outing and found them suddenly included.

He had decided things had to change, but before he'd figured out what to do, little Cindy was snatched right off the school playground. If one of the teachers hadn't blocked the small city street with her car, the kidnapper would have gotten away and done who knows what to his precious daughter. A week later, thanks to his best friend, Ray Hunter, who lived in Safe Harbor, Matt had formulated and nailed down the perfect fix to all his problems.

He'd gone to his in-laws and told them of his plan to move the girls to Safe Harbor, an hour the other side of Green Bay, up the Door Peninsula, where he'd take over for Charles Creasy as Safe Harbor's police chief.

And they'd turned on him.

They'd said he would never make it without their help. That he couldn't raise the girls alone. Then they'd gone behind his back and asked the girls if they wouldn't rather live with them and visit him on weekends. It had confused Leslie and upset the younger girls, making them all think they had to choose sides. And all because he'd wanted to raise his children in a safer environment.

And he'd been right. Here in Safe Harbor he didn't have to worry as much. Everyone knew everyone else. Tourists were welcome but noticed, as well. His girls were safer in their new town. Much safer. They'd be happy here. He'd make sure of it.

Leslie Trent stopped at the trash can between the high school and the elementary school to ditch her lunch. She'd lost fifteen pounds in two weeks. She smiled. That had to be some kind of record! She might even post it on the chat room she'd found last night. She looked around but there were too many people watching. She'd been warned on the

Web site to watch for witnesses and not to trust anyone. She'd toss the bag away in the bathroom at the station house. That would be better.

"Fatty fatty the big bad pig's her Daddy," Alan Tobridge shouted as he drove past with his friends. She hated him, and she hated this town.

But at least Alan Tobridge would have to eat his words soon. This morning after her shower she'd noticed her ribs showing in really great definition, just like the Web site promised. She was getting good definition around her hip bones, too. It was so easy. She just didn't eat. Like the Web site said, she was in control of what went into her mouth even if she had to lie and sneak around to keep that control. It was so great to be able to *do* something about a part of her life she didn't like.

Everything else might be out of her control, but this wasn't. Now all the pants she'd grown out of last year fit again, and pretty soon, when they were too big, she'd get her dad to take her shopping. He'd never notice what size she was buying. Her dad was such a man when it came to clothes.

She rolled her eyes. Lately she'd begun to think he wasn't too bright about anything. Like moving them to the sticks for a better life. Better life? The kids here looked at her like a bug under a microscope or part of an alien invasion. She hadn't made one single friend at school, but how could she tell that to her dad? Everyone loved her dad the moment they met him.

She hadn't seen Nanna and Grandpa for nearly three months, either. Not since they'd argued with her father about the move to Safe Harbor. He was dumb about that night, too. He didn't think she'd heard the things they'd said because she was in bed, but it was he who hadn't been listening. They'd said smart things like, sure, it was scary what happened to Cindy but the guy hadn't gotten away. And that her dad was leaving a great career with a great future to be a plain old cop in the sticks. All he kept saying was that she and Cindy and Gina were his kids and he'd do what he thought was best for them. And that Nanna and Grandpa had betrayed his trust. Just because they didn't agree with him and had asked the kids to live with them? When had her dad gotten so over-sensitive?

Cindy and Gina came out of the school a few minutes later. After she'd made sure they both had all the books they needed to do their homework, they walked along the footpath from the school to the police station so Daddy could drive them home.

There was a path through the woods that led to Haven Hills where their new house was, but he wouldn't let them use it. Apparently walking in the woods was too dangerous. So why did he move them to the sticks and away from Green Bay, where there were sidewalks to everywhere?

When they got to the station house, Leslie stopped at the front window to inspect her reflection. She still looked fat. Maybe another five or ten pounds would do the trick. She'd get dinner all ready again and tell Dad she'd eaten while she cooked, so she could get to her homework while he and the girls ate. He'd always believed her so far. Maybe she'd skip dinner every night. It would be worth the extra work of cooking dinner alone if she got away with skipping eating. That would have her down to one meal a day.

Good thing her dad was so out of it lately.

# Chapter Three

After delivering the Harkins children to their respective classrooms, Justine walked back to the table in the church hall where she signed up the new arrivals to After-School Days. She couldn't believe the positive response to the program. In just three weeks it had made a positive change in the community. She'd known there were several members of the Women's League and First Peninsula Church who were worried about the rising cost of after-school care, or about leaving their older children home alone or watching their younger siblings during those last hours of the workday. She'd known, but still she hadn't expected to have this many of Safe Harbor's children signed up.

A former latchkey kid herself, she knew first-hand about the loneliness of those late-afternoon hours and the pressure from peers. A house without parents was often the "party house," whether the adolescent in residence wanted it to be or not.

"This is just plain dumb, Daddy," Leslie Trent complained as the Trent clan tramped down the steps to the church hall. "You said I'm taking good care of Cindy and Gina. I'm really insulted by this."

"So you've said. I told you, sweetheart, I think you take excellent care of them. I'm just worried that you shouldn't have to. I've put too much on your shoulders lately."

"But I like taking care of them."

"Look, humor your old dad. This is the time of your life you should be enjoying yourself. Give it a couple weeks. Okay, princess?"

"Are these new participants?" Justine said, forcing herself to sound thrilled. But inside, her stomach did a quick flip, then a slow roll. She was going to have a living, breathing reminder of Matthew Trent every day—three of them, in fact. He already invaded her dreams. Broke her concentration. And worse, battered at the walls surrounding her heart with his obvious devotion to his little girls. Now she was doomed to witness the love he showed them, every day except Saturday.

*Why are You doing this to me, Lord?*

"I'm sure you remember Gina. She's in all-day kindergarten," Matt said as he put a hand lovingly on Gina's head, then moved the caress to his next-eldest child. "This is Cindy. She's in fourth grade. And last but first in the family is Leslie, who doesn't think she needs to be here."

Justine filled in the girls' sign-up sheets. "Well," she said, and took a deep calming breath, which unfortunately drew in the scent of Matt's aftershave, "I guess we'll have to do our best to change your mind, Leslie. Welcome to After-School Days, all three of you. Several of our senior citizens have volunteered to help the older kids with homework. We also got a donation of several computers, and I had high-speed Internet hooked up today so you can do research for school projects. We also have a cooperative agreement with the library. Miss Neal will be taking a group over there almost every day, so that's a possibility, too. You just have to sign up for either when you need it. Everyone will take turns."

She turned to look at the still-mutinous Leslie. "If you really like working with younger children, Leslie, several of the older high school girls have volunteered to help the younger children with homework and to assist in those rooms with general mayhem-control. I'm sure your help would be greatly appreciated."

That, at least, got a small smile from the girl. Feeling like a comedian trying to win over a tough crowd, Justine went on. "And we got a wonderful surprise today. Monica Tobridge came by and asked if I'd like her to run a cheerleading class even though she isn't a church member. The sign-up sheet is over on the bulletin board.''

"Her brother's a creep," Leslie muttered.

"Yeah. He sometimes yells mean stuff at us," Cindy put in. Leslie poked her.

"I guess it's good to know it isn't just an adult sentiment," Justine said quickly.

Matt's gaze was blazing. Young Mr. Tobridge had singled out the wrong man's children to pick on. It looked as if Alan would have another lesson taught him in the next few weeks.

"Hopefully he'll improve soon, but don't judge Monica by Alan," she told the children. "Now, your rooms will be the same as your regular Sunday school rooms. Why don't we get you settled."

"Les, will you take the girls on up. I'd like a word with Reverend Clemens," Matt said.

Justine handed each girl one of the stick-on name tags she'd written up as they talked. "Here you go, girls, you'll need to wear these just till your aide gets to know you."

"Fine, but I still say this is a dumb idea," Leslie groused as she shepherded the girls up the side steps toward the classroom wing.

"What can I do for you, Chief Trent?" she asked, trying once again for a businesslike tone.

Matt sighed as she almost knew he would. "You can stop retreating to square one each time we meet. Look, this is a new town for me and I don't know many people on a personal level. Do you have a reason not to want me for a friend?''

Ashamed instantly, she forced a little smile. "What can I do for you, *Matt?*" she corrected herself. "I'm sorry. I'm still—" Justine broke off when the radio Matt carried on his hip squawked to life. There was a huge accident out on Route 7, the state highway nearest Safe Harbor. Some of the victims were pinned in their cars.

"I've got to go. I know it's an imposition, but if I can't get back in time, could you make sure the girls get home okay? Les knows to make our neighbors, the Hunters, aware that they're alone. I went to college with both of them, and I trust them with the kids. Ray and Julie were the ones who put me on to the opening for Chief of Police here in Safe Harbor. This has never happened before, but I set it up with them in case of emergencies like this. Knowing the house next door to theirs was up for sale made the move here all the more attractive."

Justine nodded, relieved that she didn't have to answer his question, yet embarrassed by the cause. "I'll see the children get home. Don't worry. Just go. The accident sounds dreadful."

After he left, Justine floated from age group to age group, checking on how the senior citizens who'd volunteered were getting along with the children. Everything seemed to be going fine so she returned to her makeshift desk to find Leslie just leaving the kitchen area.

"Oh, hi, Reverend Clemens," the girl said, her hands fluttering nervously. "I was just…uh… getting a drink. Helping the little kids is kind of fun. Well, see ya."

Justine frowned as she watched Leslie skip up the steps on her way back to the classroom wing. There were water fountains in the halls. Why hadn't Leslie used one of them? She walked into the kitchen and looked around. There was a paper lunch bag in a trash can—a can Justine had emptied after the women's altar guild left earlier in the day.

She dismissed the whole incident until the next day. As she checked the building before locking up, Justine got an impulse to check the trash: once again, there was a lunch bag in the can. It contained a sandwich, an apple and some carrot sticks. She wished she'd checked the one the day before because this time she found the initials *LT* on the bottom. *Leslie Trent?* Why would the girl throw out her lunch?

The same thing happened for the next two days, and Justine's curiosity turned to concern. Matt's daughter was secretly disposing of her lunches.

Deeply troubled, Justine thought back to the first time she'd seen the girl during the summer. There was no denying that Matt's eldest child was increasingly fragile looking. Justine had thought the girl was just getting taller and losing baby fat, but now she was afraid it was more. Something was wrong, and these lunch bags were a clue.

It took another day to put her finger on what. When Justine pulled yet another bag from the trash on Friday, she remembered an article she'd read in a ministry periodical on eating disorders.

How was she going to tell Matt there was a chance his daughter was suffering from anorexia?

It was Friday, and Matt was looking forward to a whole weekend off. He'd managed to plow through a mountain of backed-up paperwork and was out of work an hour earlier than usual. It was a beautiful afternoon. All day he thought about taking the girls for a short hike up at Safe Harbor Park, and there was still enough light left to do so. Russ Mitchard said the park had the best wilderness trails on the peninsula.

Matt had just cleared the front door of the church building when he ran into Justine. Literally. He managed to catch her before she fell. Her scent surrounded him and she felt wonderful in his arms as she stared up at him with an expression he couldn't decipher.

"I'm…uh…I'm so sorry," she said, stepping back, giving him no choice but to let her go.

"Not your fault I came barreling in here and knocked you for a loop. I was in a hurry to pick

up the girls. I thought we'd go for a hike before
the light fails."

"Oh. But I really need to talk to you."

The disappointment in Justine's face gave him
a shot of pleasure. "So come with us." The words
had just popped out of his mouth. Too late, he
noticed her outfit. She wasn't really dressed for a
hike. She had on a long top and slacks made of a
velvety soft material that was pretty but casual.

"I...no, you don't understand. I need to talk
about Leslie."

Confusion assailed him along with a sense of
disappointment that she only wanted to talk to him
about his daughter. "Leslie? Is she not settling in?
She said this was working out okay."

"As far as I know it is. She's been getting on
just fine. It isn't that she's any trouble." Justine
paused. "It's something else. Have you noticed her
losing weight lately? A lot of weight?"

Matt frowned. What was she getting at? "Les is
getting taller, that's all. Her clothes still fit, so she
couldn't have lost weight. You wouldn't know this
because you don't have kids, but every once in a
while they shoot up and look thinner. I guess they
don't grow everything at once. At her age, I grew
six inches in one summer and didn't gain an ounce.
I could hardly keep my pants up."

Justine didn't crack a smile. He watched as she
took a deep breath. "Matt, I've found her lunch in
the trash four days in a row. Earlier today when I

asked her why, she said she doesn't like what you pack but doesn't want to hurt your feelings.''

Leslie normally packed all of the lunches, but he wasn't about to tell Justine that. She seemed to be implying he wasn't taking good care of his kids. Or that they were afraid to speak their minds.

Brother. He was batting a thousand lately. First Mary and Seth, two people he'd thought of as parents since marrying their daughter, had begun doubting his ability to raise the girls without their mother and criticizing his every decision. And now the first person he'd been attracted to since Diane's death was calling him an incompetent parent.

''Leslie can say anything to me she wants,'' he growled. ''And she knows it. If she'd said she wanted something else for lunch, I'd have seen she had it.''

''I have no doubt of that. I don't think she wants something else for lunch. In fact, Gina told me it's Leslie who makes the lunches.''

''I don't appreciate your questioning my children, Reverend.''

Justine stiffened. It was as if he saw a barrier form around her.

''I didn't question Gina, *Chief Trent*. She offered the information in one of her sweet, running advertisements for a mother. I came to you with a concern for your child. Not to inspire an attack on my motives. I'm terribly afraid Leslie may have an eating disorder.''

Matt shook his head. There was nothing wrong with his Leslie. She was losing her baby fat. And she'd gotten taller. Hadn't he said that already?

Justine stepped forward and put her hand on his forearm. He could see her concern for Leslie in her eyes and hear it in her voice.

"I'm not criticizing. A blind man could see how much you love those girls. But you can't afford to be blind to their faults and problems. Matt, please don't discount what I'm saying. Watch her. Carefully. If I'm right, and I pray I'm not, this can be very dangerous. Anorexia is insidious and it's a silent killer."

"Leslie's fine," he insisted.

Before Justine could once again rebut his assertion, the clamor of little feet sounded down the hall from the classroom wing.

Minutes later he had both the little ones with him and watched Leslie strolling along the hall and down the steps. All at once she looked so alone to him. Maybe watching her closely wouldn't be such a bad idea. After all, the girls were in this program because he'd been worried about Les.

As they started to put dinner together, Matt made it a point to notice if Leslie really did pick at what they were making for dinner. He felt guilty and almost sneaky. As if he were spying on her.

"Don't you like dinner, Les?" he felt compelled to ask when he noticed how little of her meal she was actually eating. They all sat around the big maple table Diane had so lovingly restored. As far as Diane had been concerned, family meals were the center of the universe.

"Dinner's fine, Daddy. But ham is a little fattening. I just don't want to be fat. That's all."

That was the first he'd heard that she was worried about her weight. Maybe there *was* something here he needed to address. And maybe she *had* lost a little weight along with the inches she'd gained. On the walk, he had noticed Les just sort of floated along with a growing grace that made his heart ache and made him aware that his little girl was headed inexorably toward womanhood.

"Are you on a diet, princess?" he asked casually.

She shrugged. "Not really. I just like my clothes to fit loose. You know. Grandma's no lightweight, either. When I get older, if I already eat right, I won't have to worry that I'll look like her. And I can look like the models in *Pizzazz* and *Mystique*."

Matt sighed. America—a plastic surgeon's paradise! Where men were supposed to be overmuscled and women were starting to look the same except for their out-of-proportion breasts.

"You know all those women don't really look like that naturally, don't you? Some have surgery and most of their photos are retouched."

That got Leslie's attention. Her head snapped up. "You think so?"

"Oh. Yeah. I saw it on a TV show about special effects. A graphic artist trims thighs, arms, hips, whatever the photographer wants slimmed down with the computer. It's all smoke and mirrors. Your mother never dieted. She just ate healthy and let the good Lord take care of how she looked. And she looked wonderful. You will, too."

Leslie tilted her head and frowned, clearly thinking about what he'd said. "You thought Mom was pretty?"

He could think of Diane now and remember her before the cancer. He smiled and knew it had a wistful quality. But that was okay. He'd never hidden his grief from the kids. They knew he missed their mom as much as they did. "She was perfect. Didn't you think so?"

Her eyes shone and she nodded. "She was. Wasn't she? Thanks, Daddy," she told him with a sweet broad smile.

Matt gave a sigh of relief. Leslie was going to be fine. Justine had just panicked. Now all he had to do was apologize to the pretty minister for putting her in the crosshairs of his insecurities over single parenthood. He couldn't believe how he'd spoken to her. And all because she cared about his daughter.

# *Chapter Four*

Justine heard footsteps in the hall coming toward her office. She looked up from the lesson she'd prepared for her newly instituted Wednesday night youth service. While she was ready for a visitor, she wasn't ready to find Chief Matthew Trent and his wide shoulders filling her doorway.

The quickened beat of her heart told her a forewarning probably wouldn't have helped, anyway. To see Matt was to—and oh, how she hated admitting this even to herself—desire him. That he was in uniform didn't help. What was it about men in uniform? And why didn't being a minister exempt her from those kind of thoughts? They were entirely inappropriate, and besides that, embarrassing and inconvenient!

"Got a minute?" Matt asked, and Justine felt

immediate contrition. The man was clearly troubled.

"Come in. What can I do for you?"

"A couple things, actually," he said, sinking into the chair across from her desk. "I've been meaning to get over here to see you ever since Friday but, with one thing and another going on, my time's been a little tight."

"I noticed the girls weren't at Sunday school. Frankly, I worried that I'd chased you all away."

"Of course you didn't chase us away. Gina was up sick all night Saturday, so we slept in. The reason I wanted to see you is to say I was wrong to snap at you on Friday. I'd like to apologize. You were just concerned for Les, and I overreacted instead of being appreciative that you'd worry about her."

He raked a hand through his shock of dark hair. "I'm afraid I'm a little sensitive about the girls. I made the mistake of leaning heavily on my in-laws after Diane died. Then, when Cindy was taken—"

"Taken?"

Matt sat back and crossed his ankle over his knee. "I assumed you knew what prompted our move here. Cindy was snatched from the playground at school last spring."

Justine's hand flew to cover her heart. "Oh dear Lord. That's horrible."

He closed his eyes for a few seconds as if to banish the horror, then opened them and nodded.

''We got lucky. A teacher who'd had Cindy in a previous grade happened to be leaving for a doctor's appointment. She saw Cindy in the car crying. She knew me, and since I wasn't the driver, she decided to make sure everything was all right. She drove her car across the street and blocked his car in. Better safe than sorry, she thought, and, of course, she was right. One of the male teachers saw what was happening, saw the vehicle turn around, and chased it on foot, hoping to get the plate number, at least. When the car had to stop, he managed to get the door open with Cindy's help and pulled her out. The perp fled on foot, but the police had him in custody within the hour.''

''You must have been terrified for her.''

Matt nodded. ''And that's why I decided to move somewhere safer. My in-laws weren't so understanding. They live about an hour the other side of Green Bay. Seth's seventy now. He was never much of a driver, but now he hates driving through the city or on high-speed highways. And, of course, they'd gotten used to stopping in every day. I know this is a long drive, but they acted as if Safe Harbor were the dark side of the moon. I'd asked their opinion on so much for so long, they must have begun to think they had a right to dictate how and where I should raise the girls. They wanted me to keep my job with the FBI and have the girls live with them, visiting on weekends. I couldn't even consider that.''

"After losing their mother, that would have been disastrous for them."

Matt moved in his chair, visibly restless and tense. "That's how I felt. Anyway, Ray called about the job in Safe Harbor, and I decided the move here would be better for all concerned. My in-laws objected and even told the girls their alternative solution without consulting me."

"I can't think that was right, and I, for one, think you made the right decision. As I said, the girls didn't need to lose you as well as their mother."

"Not to hear their grandparents tell it. They don't think I'm capable of raising three girls alone."

Justine could hear the hurt in his voice.

"Well, anyway," he continued, "I'm proud of my relationship with my kids. We're close. There's nothing I wouldn't do for them. Nothing's more important to me than they are. I'm a good father." A note of uncertainty entered his voice.

"Of course, you are. I never doubted that for a moment," she assured him.

"Right now, *I* am. Doubting me, I mean. Sort of, anyway." He shook his head and sat straighter, dropping the relaxed cross-legged posture. "I don't know. I thought I'd solved any problem with Leslie's eating on Friday night. She admitted to watching her diet so she wouldn't gain weight in her adult years. Diane's mother is a little on the plump side, and I think it may have had Les worried. But then we had a long talk about dieting and the reality of retouched fashion magazine photos. She seemed to understand. Then last night, I caught her tossing her dinner in the trash.

"I confronted her about it, and before I knew it we were in a raging, door-slamming battle. She hates it here. Hates me for bringing her here. She should have stayed with Seth and Mary. She called me 'stupid' and 'selfish' among other things, the kindest of which was 'dictator.' She apologized later but..." He grimaced.

The man was heartbroken. "But you thought you were her hero and it hurts that she's coming to see things about you she characterizes as faults."

Matt blinked and stared at her. "How did you know that?"

"I'm smarter than the average minister because I'm a woman," she teased, shooting him a grin.

The teasing did no good. Matt was just too upset to unwind that easily. "One of the things she really unloaded about is that practically every minute we're together has something to do with chores. She's right. Between trying to get completely moved in—my garage is still wall-to-wall boxes—and all the everyday things Diane would have handled while I was at work..." He sighed. "She told me later that she was just angry but... Justine, I'm not sure she meant it. I thought I knew my daughter.''

"I'm sure you do. More than the average male parent of a thirteen-year-old girl. It's a very difficult period. So much changes in that year. I often feel sorry for those ninth graders. They don't really belong in the junior high building nor the high school building. She's growing up, Matt, and unfortunately that means growing away, as well. It's a natural, albeit painful, process.''

Matt scrubbed his hand over his face. "I wish I were sure that's all there is to it. Listen, I know it's an imposition, but would you mind coming over for dinner one night soon and just sort of observing her? Maybe you'll see something I'm missing. And maybe if she hears another woman in an informal setting talking about this dieting idea, she'll see she's going at it all wrong.''

Justine really didn't think she'd be able to help, but didn't want to close the door with a refusal. "It isn't an imposition at all. I'm always here for the kids and their parents. Besides, it'll save me cooking for myself at least one night.''

"Would tonight be too soon?"

"No. Tonight would be fine.''

He smiled broadly, his relief palpable. "Thanks.''

At six-thirty sharp, Justine pulled up in the Trents' driveway and took a moment to send a quick prayer heavenward that she wouldn't misstep.

She was only halfway up the walk when the front door flew open and Cindy and Gina spilled out with Matt trailing behind.

"Don't knock the poor woman over, girls," he called after them, as they both barreled into her, shooting greetings and queries a mile a minute. She put her arms around both girls and tried to answer.

"Now, let me see. Yes, I'd love to see your room, Cindy. And, yes, I'd love to meet your friend Binky," she said, carefully taking a baby blanket that had seen better days. It seemed the most natural thing in the world to smooth it over her hand and turn it quickly into a puppet.

"Hello, Reverend Clemens," she said, giving Binky a squeaky voice. "Hello to you, too, Binky," she answered, quickly changing back to her own voice. "Gina's my person. We're very good friends," Binky replied.

Gina giggled and took Binky back, clumsily fashioning the puppet around her own hand. "Will you be my friend, too, and maybe stay overnight? We have bunk beds. We'll share. Won't we, Gina?"

"Sure," Gina continued in the high-pitched voice she'd assigned to Binky, then quickly corrected the tone, and giggled, saying "Sure" again in her own register.

Matt cleared his throat. "I don't think, Reverend Clemens could—"

"I really can't," Justine said at the same moment. They both laughed in shared camaraderie and chagrin.

"Girls, let's get inside before dinner burns...or our guest runs for her life," Matt put in, after scooping Gina and Binky up in his arms.

He'd promised to fix ravioli in a red meat sauce that he called gravy, a term he said he'd learned from his Italian grandmother. His Mediterranean background wasn't a surprise to Justine. His deep brown eyes, dark complexion and nearly black hair told an unmistakable tale of Latin roots.

Justine followed the crowd inside the farmhouse-design home. She found it a pleasant surprise after the way Matt had described the state of his garage. The living room was beautifully arranged. If the rest of his home looked as put together, she would know he'd been exaggerating.

"Matt, this is lovely. You have a real talent for decorating."

A snort came from behind and to the left. Justine turned and found Leslie leaning in the doorway of a softly lit room next to the staircase. "Like Dad knows more than how to stuff a room full of furniture."

"Les told me where to put what, what color to paint the walls and what to hang where," Matt confessed. "Otherwise, nothing would have been hung up and the furniture would be arranged like a doctor's waiting room. My back still aches thinking about moving everything around till my slave-driver daughter was satisfied.''

Mindful that a lack of self-esteem was reported to be a prime cause of eating disorders, Justine jumped on the chance to bolster Leslie's sense of self. ''You have quite a talent, Leslie. Maybe someday you'll be an interior designer.''

The teen shrugged shyly. ''Mom bought it all. I just said where to put it. And the paint color was common sense. It was no big deal.''

''Oh, you're wrong. Really. It takes the right eye to know how to arrange things this nicely. And color is so easily off a shade. I know grown women who can't do this well. Unfortunately, I head the list. Maybe you could lend me that eye of yours someday, if it's all right with your dad. I hate the way my place is coming together. As your dad said, it looks like a doctor's waiting room with the furniture lined up along the walls.''

Again Leslie shrugged, but she did stand a little straighter and taller. ''Yeah. Sure. I could help.''

''I guess that means I'll be moving furniture again,'' Matt said, giving a deep theatrical sigh.

Leslie rolled her eyes. ''Oh, Daddy,'' she said with the kind of exaggerated disgust only a thir-teen-year-old can do justice to.

Justine laughed. ''So, where's this authentic Italian dinner I was promised?''

Matt tucked the younger girls in bed and settled Les down at the computer in her room to finish the rest of her homework. Then, somewhat reluctantly, he headed back to the family room where Justine waited. He watched her lovely face in silent repose reflected in the window as she stared out at the darkened sky and took a sip of the tea he'd given her before going off to see to the girls.

For a moment Matt found himself unable to move—held in check by Justine's beauty. But, he reminded himself, he needed something of more substance from this woman—this minister—than her captivating loveliness. With his daughter's happiness at stake, attraction took a back seat to answers. Answers he needed but feared.

Matt took a deep fortifying breath before plunging ahead into troubled waters. If she said something negative, he didn't know how he'd handle it. There was nothing more important to him than being the best of fathers. What would he do if he'd failed?

"Everyone's all settled," he told her before losing his nerve.

Justine turned and smiled, but there was a hint of nervousness in her expression. "Matt," she said, almost as if she were surprised to see him there.

"Oh-oh. You spotted a problem, didn't you? I don't relish hearing you tell me I'm a failure as a father, but—"

Justine's eyes widened. "Goodness, Matt, you're

nothing of the sort. I was just going over something troubling in my mind. And it had little to do with your situation. Those girls adore you—even Leslie, as angry as you say she was with you. Her eyes simply shine when she looks at you. I've just been wondering if you'd ever considered hiring a part-time housekeeper to do light housework around here and to, perhaps, cook dinner?''

"Actually, I did. Just after Diane passed away. But her mother was afraid a stranger coming in and doing the things Diane used to do would upset the girls. It made sense at the time," he added, not wanting Justine to think he was rejecting her idea out of hand.

"It may have been a mistake then but I think the two of you have carried this burden long enough. Watching Leslie tonight, I couldn't help but think she might feel as overwhelmed as you do. Leslie's still just a child. She tries so very hard to be helpful. Almost too hard."

"She's been like that ever since Diane got sick. Mary was around a lot more then, but even so, Les pitched right in to fill in the gaps. Are you saying you think that's a bad thing?"

"I don't honestly know. I can't see that learning to handle responsibility is a bad thing, but maybe too much could be overwhelming. You did say she complained about all your activities together centering around chores. As I said, I have no way of knowing what she's thinking, so I could be wrong.

But I did a lot of filling in for my mother at Leslie's age and I never stopped eating as Les seems to have.'' Justine shrugged as if to admit that kids were baffling.

Les was his problem. He didn't want to burden the pretty preacher overly much, and she seemed so concerned. ''That's the trouble with parenthood,'' he said, walking away to drop into his favorite chair. ''Kids don't come with instructions written on their bottoms.''

Justine chuckled as he'd meant her to and joined him, sitting on the love seat next to his chair. ''And all the books written on the subject contradict each other.''

''Exactly. So you think a housekeeper might help?''

''I don't see how it could hurt.''

Neither did he, but he didn't know that many people in Safe Harbor yet and he hated relying on Ray any more than he already had. Both Ray and Julie had done so much for him and the girls already. He couldn't have them looking for a housekeeper, too.

''I actually have someone in mind,'' Justine was saying, coming to his rescue. ''You might know her. Elizabeth Neal. She was Safe Harbor's postmistress until she retired. Elizabeth is alone in the world, so she fills her life with activities like singing in the choir, organizing the town's Harvest Fest and cooking for the needy. She actually complained last week that the Harvest Festival wasn't the trouble it used to be. She's done it so often and has it so well organized that it practically puts itself on. She told me that for the first time in her life she's sorry she never married. I think she's lonely and missing having the children and grandchildren her friends enjoy so much."

"I think I know her. Yeah. The Harvest Fest Lady. Short? White hair? Real grandmotherly looking and always smiling?"

"That's Elizabeth. I'll bet she'd even be glad to fill in with the girls on days when you have to work and it doesn't coincide with school or the After-School Days program. She's seventy, but I'm sure she'd be able to do this with one hand tied behind her back. The woman wears me out at the church. Just don't ask her to sew anything. You might not like the results."

Matt shrugged, not about to let a possible gem slip through his fingers over a few stitches. "That's what the tailor shop is for. Lead me to this wonder," he all but begged. This was for the girls, and Elizabeth Neal sounded like the missing piece of a puzzle—a perfect fit.

# Chapter Five

By lunchtime the next day, Matt was so psyched he couldn't wait to tell the girls. He glanced at his watch when he heard Justine's voice as she made her way down the hall.

"So, how did it go?" she asked as she entered the room.

"Thanks for letting me borrow your office. It's a lot friendlier than asking her to stop by the station house for a talk after she finished choir practice."

Justine let out a bark of laughter, then quickly covered her mouth, her soft brown eyes widening in surprise. "Oh. I'm sorry. That just sounded so funny."

Matt smiled. "Another one of my questionable jokes. You're the only one who gets them." He wondered what her reaction would be if he told her he thought she was sweet and kind and almost irresistibly adorable when she deviated from her ministerial persona.

"How did it go with Elizabeth?" she asked again.

"She's thrilled with the offer and will be glad to do a little light work around the house and take care of the girls, as long as she can fit it in around her normal activities. We're going to give it a shot and see how it works out. She's willing to give me between twelve and twenty hours a week. She also knows someone who'd be willing to do the heavy cleaning, like floors and bathrooms. If she charges what Elizabeth says, I can easily budget for both."

"That's wonderful. I hope it helps Leslie," Justine said, and shot him a wide smile that he felt to his toes.

"Even if it doesn't settle her down at all, it'll sure help me. Sometimes I just get so tired of having to be *on* 24/7." He glanced at his watch. "Say. It's just about time for lunch. How about I thank you for your help with a quick meal at Harry's Kitchen?"

"I don't know," she said, looking unsure and glancing at her desk.

"You have to eat, anyway, and Harry's Kitchen is always a nice change of pace. Of course, there's no telling what he'll have on the menu."

She chuckled. "Menu? You mean what he

bought this morning at the grocery store to serve today. Eating there is always an experience. Okay. Let's go." She plucked her purse off the coat tree in the corner and tossed it over her shoulder.

Matt followed her out the door. "I notice you didn't say what kind of experience."

Justine's laughter floated after her.

Harry's was crowded when Justine and Matt got there, but Harry waved them to the last booth. It was the "Reserved" booth Harry kept for the use of select customers. Since she wasn't one of that august group, Justine assumed Matt was.

"You want coffee?" Matt asked when she sat. At her nod, Matt went behind the counter, scooted by Harry who was at the register and filled two mismatched mugs. Customers were usually expected to pour their own coffee and juice, get their own silverware and clear their own tables—all because that's the way Harry ran the place. There were clever signs tacked all over, telling everyone that's the only way they were going to get fed quickly. There weren't menus, either. You asked for it, and if Harry had it, he made it.

The place was a Safe Harbor landmark, as was Harry Connell, a retired merchant marine who didn't stand on ceremony. The little diner's walls were paneled halfway up with gray weathered barn wood and painted a cheerful yellow the rest of the way to the ceiling. At some point he must have acquired endless bolts of green vinyl to upholster the booths and counter stools, because if one was damaged, the next day it was repaired with more of the same material. The tables and the counter behind which Harry held court as he cooked were fifties-era gray marble-patterned Formica. Everything behind the counter was stainless steel and gleaming.

"You certainly get royal treatment. Harry's reserved booth, no less," she teased, as Matt put down her coffee and dumped a handful of creamers on the table.

He chuckled. "One of the perks of the job. They didn't bother to list it, but it might have made my decision easier."

"In that case, I'll have to eat with you more often." Justine could have bitten her tongue right off. Her face heated and she began studying the contents of her purse.

"Now, there's a possibility to make a man look forward to Harry's every day. It's a deal." Matt checked his watch. "I'll see you here at twelve-thirty tomorrow, then."

"I was only kidding," she said, more flustered than ever.

He looked crestfallen. "Oh. And here I thought I'd discovered the cure to afternoon indigestion."

"First off, Harry only serves sandwiches at lunch, and, appearances to the contrary, he's a wonderful cook."

Matt gave a dramatic sigh and leaned back. "Found out. Truth is, it's a little lonely eating by myself every day. I could eat in my office, but I come in here to stay visible and accessible. People will often stop to lodge a minor complaint that I doubt they'd ever call or stop at the station to talk over. I've always thought irritations were more easily solved than altercations."

"That's a very wise policy."

"But it's still lonely. Lately my conversations either revolve around schoolwork with the girls or who bought the Harbor Quay apartment buildings. Everyone has an opinion on what's going on with all the renovations at the complex, and they all want me to investigate. One person swears it's the mafia come to destroy our town." He grinned appealingly and took a sip of his coffee. "So, are you going to take pity on me?"

What could she say? More importantly, what did she want to say? Matt wanted a friend, he'd said. He'd made no romantic gestures, so she doubted he shared her attraction for him. That made friendship with him safe because she had no intention of ever becoming romantically involved with a man, no matter how trustworthy he seemed. Her father had been a war hero and had still destroyed her mother's life with his desertion. So what harm could a few lunches and a little companionship cause?

"I'm afraid I'm one of those people frequently

involved in working lunches. The church's women often have luncheon meetings, and as head of women's ministries, I'm required to attend if invited. Also, like constituent complaints for you, counseling for me often works better over a nice friendly meal. But still, I'm usually free a couple times a week.''

"Tomorrow?"

"Sorry. I'm not free for lunch again until next Thursday."

"Then, it's a date. Twelve-thirty next Thursday."

*A date!* If only those two little words hadn't shot a bolt of need through her. If only they didn't thrill her. If only they didn't fill her with dread.

What was she going to do about these feelings Matthew Trent provoked in her?

Justine pulled her hand back from the receiver she'd just carefully replaced. Why now, after all these years, would her father contact her? Hadn't she made something of herself in spite of the shambles in which George Clemens left her world? In spite of the shambles she herself had made of her adolescence.

What did he really want? What drove a man to walk out on his wife, his five-year-old daughter and all his responsibilities, then, twenty-six years later, appear out of the blue? She didn't believe for a moment his claim that he just wanted to hear her voice, catch up on her life and perhaps see her eventually. A man didn't reappear after two decades. He just didn't!

Or, at least, he shouldn't expect to.

The big grandfather clock in the hall bonged the half-hour, bringing Justine out of her troubled thoughts. Twelve-thirty. There was something she was supposed to do at twelve-thirty. The second her eyes fell on her desk-blotter calendar she remembered. Lunch with Matt.

She'd been reluctant to keep the appointment, but now, with her emotions all astir, she knew she should beg off. The problem was, it was already too late. She couldn't cancel because Harry only had a pay phone at his little eatery—another of the ex-merchant marine's idiosyncracies. That meant she had to at least make an appearance and cancel in person, or Matt might waste his lunchtime waiting for her.

With little enthusiasm, she left for Harry's. She could tell Matt something had come up and leave, but that would be a lie and she refused to let his persistence goad her into lying. That wouldn't honor her Lord or her position in His church.

Justine opened the glass door to Harry's a few minutes later and spied Matt right away. He stood at the counter talking to Felicity Smith. He was frowning down at the young single mother. Justine assumed he was listening to one of the little complaints he'd told her his presence at Harry's often brought to the light. Even so, she felt something dark move across her heart. Jealousy? Ridiculous. Friends didn't feel jealousy.

Matt looked up when the bell on the door tinkled. His frown smoothed out and his eyes lit as a smile curved his lips. Justine's heart did a flip in her chest. Friends didn't feel emotions like that, either. This wasn't good.

He said one last thing to Felicity, who nodded and then twirled her stool back toward the counter. Matt left her side and walked toward Justine.

"You want coffee or tea?" he asked.

Somewhere between her office and Matt's magnetic grin, Justine realized she'd changed her mind. Lunch with Matt was exactly what she needed, though she had to admit she didn't know why. There was every indication that nice and trustworthy as he seemed, Matt was going to wreak havoc in her life.

"I'll have coffee, but it's my turn to serve. You sit. I bet you do a lot more physical work in a day than I do."

Matt shrugged and smiled. "Never let it be said I turn down a pretty lady bent on waiting on me. Pour away with the coffee. I'm working late tonight."

Less than a minute later Justine joined Matt with cups filled and creamers at the ready. "So, how are the girls?"

"The little ones are great. They love Elizabeth. But believe it or not, Leslie seems to resent her."

"Oh, I'm so sorry. I don't seem to be much help where she's concerned."

Matt shook his head and sat back into the corner of the booth. He kept his arm outstretched along the table and absently stirred his coffee. "Don't feel that way. I think you were right. This last week since Elizabeth started has been wonderful. I've stuck to my guns. Leslie's under orders to be polite. Even if she wasn't overwhelmed with work before Elizabeth started with us, I was. And so was Cindy. Gina told me she'd missed me—as if I hadn't been there all along. I want time to enjoy my kids, and I want them to enjoy their childhood. It's over fast enough as it is."

Justine nodded and wondered what her life might have been like if she'd had the kind of childhood Matt was determined to give his girls. What if she'd had a father like Matthew Trent? A mother who hadn't been involved with an endless parade of men, each a less acceptable father figure than the last? She wondered what it would have been like to be cherished as Leslie, Cindy and Gina were, instead of being tolerated, exploited as a housekeeper in her own home, then shunted aside when her plans for the future didn't agree with her mother's.

She'd have been a less angry, a less troubled teen. Even now, she might be a different person.

Justine frowned. The trouble with all this speculation was that she *liked* who she was and where she'd ended up in life. Her difficult childhood had made her the woman she was.

That didn't absolve her father, though. Nothing would.

Justine jolted back to the here and now when Matt took her hand and dropped several coins in her palm. He'd sat straight and had turned to face her.

"What's this?" she asked, wishing the table were wider and that he wasn't so close she could smell the clean, fresh aroma of his aftershave.

"All the change in my pocket. I figured thoughts as deep as the ones you're mulling over must be worth a lot more than a penny. Anything you can talk about without breaking the confidence of a parishioner?"

Once again, Matt presented her with the perfect opportunity to stay in the self-imposed bubble of privacy where she'd lived her past ten years. All she had to do was lie. But she'd already admitted that would be wrong. Besides, something about Matt made her want to reach out and confront her worries and fears. Maybe it was his bravery in the face of dealing with grief over his wife's death and raising his girls alone.

"My father called me earlier."

Matt raised an eyebrow. "And that's a problem?"

Justine looked at her hands as she fumbled with a sugar packet. "Actually, it is. Every father isn't as dedicated and loving as you are. I think I mentioned that my mother wasn't an ideal parent. And that I had to pick up a lot of slack for her when I was young. And I know I mentioned the way I rebelled as a teen until Reverend Burns took me under his wing."

"The liberty spike hair! As the father of three girls, that image sure scared ten years off my life," he said with a smile that she instinctively knew was designed to make her relax. When she didn't react, Matt continued, his voice full of understanding and compassion. "Your father was no better, I gather?"

"As bad as Mother was, my father was worse and the cause of all the problems," she told him, trying not to sound as bitter as she still felt. "When I was five years old, he didn't go to work one day. She often talked about how his boss called looking for him and how she had no idea where he was. That day he simply disappeared and left us floundering. Financially and emotionally. He broke Mother's heart and her spirit. She wasn't cut out to be alone, and over the years there were quite a few men in our lives. Each was more worthless than the last."

"I'm sorry. What did your father want when he called this morning?"

"To connect. To catch up. To explain. I could

scarcely listen. He said he'd call again when I was more used to the idea of talking to him. I said that would be okay, because I couldn't think what else to say." She stared at her hands. They were balled together, a tight bundle of tensed muscle and bone that she couldn't seem to untangle. She looked up and blinked back the tears that threatened. "I don't want him to call. I don't want to talk to him. What explanation could there be for what he did?"

"I can't think of one, but your father apparently feels there is one or he wouldn't have contacted you."

"I'm so close to hating that man. I'm a minister of the Lord. I'm not supposed to hate. Especially my own father."

"Hey. You're still human, and it's human nature to feel hatred toward those who've hurt us. I have a little experience in the paternal hate area myself. It's one of the reasons being a good father is so important to me. My father and I had one of the worst relationships a father and son can have. He was never there when I needed him. If I had a problem, his advice as he flew out the door for another important meeting was to suck it up and deal with whatever it was on my own."

She watched as Matt stirred his coffee absently, his eyes avoiding hers, staring out the window.

"My mother had died by the time I graduated college, and Diane and I got married in July the same year. Di didn't even know my father was still alive. One day a social worker from a local hospital tracked me down. My father had had a severe heart attack and was asking for me. I refused to go see him. Diane insisted my refusal proved I still had emotions wrapped up in him. She said I had to deal with those feelings before I could ever hope to be a decent father to our own children. She all but hog-tied me to get me there.

"I went. He was weak but able to talk. He said he regretted being the same kind of father *he'd* had. Then he begged me to learn what was really important from the mistakes he'd made, and not repeat them. It turned out he wanted to see me to insure my happiness. It had very little to do with him, though he did ask for forgiveness. He lived for a few more days, and we managed to make peace. I'll be forever grateful to Di for that. And to my dad."

Justine leaned forward. "But at least your father was a presence in your life while you were growing up. He didn't run off and leave you and your mother to your own devices."

Matt grimaced. "No. He didn't. Our situations *are* different in that way. But I will tell you something I've learned being a parent. Parents are just people. People who make a lot of mistakes. Unfortunately, those mistakes often adversely affect their children. Maybe if those children weren't so dependent on them and busy forming their personalities while the mistakes were being made it wouldn't matter so much. But, of course, it does matter. A lot.''

''That makes sense.'' Justine twisted her napkin before patting it flat on the table. ''My father's mistakes certainly hurt me, and they're responsible for some of my attitudes.''

''How can listening to him hurt you more than wondering for the rest of your life why he left? I think you owe it to yourself to find out. One day it'll be too late.''

''I can't. I just can't.'' The napkin fell to the floor. ''There are too many years and too much hurt piled up for me to deal with him.''

Matt shrugged. ''It's your decision. I just hope it's the right one.''

Justine sighed, suddenly very tired. ''Me, too.''

''Hey, you two. You ordering or just takin' up room?'' Harry shouted over the counter at them. His iron-gray hair was mussed as usual and his apron was probably the best representation of the day's menu to be found.

After telling Harry what they wanted and adjusting their wants to his current supply, they looked at each other and laughed. ''It doesn't do to have your mind set on something specific, does it?'' she said, then sobered. ''I find I can't eat a meal anymore and not think of Leslie. Have you thought more about the whole eating issue with her?''

''I'm watching her more carefully and making

sure she eats her breakfast and dinner. There isn't much I can do about lunch. I spoke with the school nurse, and she said she'd have a talk with her—but that just made Les as mad as a wet hen.''

''I've done some reading on the subject, Matt,'' Justine said, glad that the conversation about her father had ended. ''Everything I see indicates anorexia has less to do with food than the layperson thinks, and more to do with psychological problems. I really think you should get some advice from a professional trained to handle a dangerous problem like this.''

''I'm not convinced she even has an eating disorder.''

Justine looked up with a start to see that Harry was standing next to their table with the food. She smiled as she took her plate and Harry refilled her cup before leaving.

''My point is, neither you nor I nor the school nurse are really trained to know. But there is a clinic right in Green Bay that specializes in eating disorders.''

Matt hesitated before taking a bite of his sandwich, then put it down. ''So I'd just take her there and they'd tell me if she is anorexic and how to handle her?''

''Actually, they usually admit patients. They feel the treatment they offer is too difficult and the consequences of the disease are too severe to let families handle it on their own.''

Matt's chin rose and firmed stubbornly. "I'm not turning my kid over to strangers. Who knows what kind of things they might do to her? And she may just be going through a dieting phase and be doing it in a way that isn't smart."

"I know it would be difficult."

He shook his head. "Try impossible. I won't place my trust in anyone else where my kids are concerned."

Justine blinked. "Anyone?" she asked softly. "What about God? Just ask Him to guide your decisions where Leslie is concerned. You trust *Him*, don't you?"

Matthew frowned. "I don't think I do. I guess there are still some effects of my father in my life. And from losing Di, too. My father was never there for me. I couldn't trust him. Then I loved Diane, and God still let her die. I let my in-laws into my heart, and the minute I didn't do exactly as they wanted, they turned on me. No. Trust is a little beyond me right now. Especially in God. And I certainly can't trust strangers with Les. I just can't."

"You're wrong about God. I pray you see that soon. And about the clinic. What if she needs their help?"

"Look, I can see you're really concerned and I appreciate it. Suppose I take her to her pediatrician back in Green Bay. He's known Les from the day she was born. He'll know if there's a real problem or if she just needs a little education on dieting.''

Justine nodded. ''It's a step in the right direction, I suppose. He's at least a doctor. All we are is a couple of worried adults wandering through articles on the Internet.'' She glanced at her watch, looking uncomfortable. ''I'd better gobble my lunch and get going. I have a meeting at half-past one.''

Minutes later Matt said goodbye to Justine outside Harry's Kitchen and walked along Market Square to the station house. Lunch had been a big mistake. He'd decided to move on. To refuse to feel guilty for seeking companionship from a woman other than Diane. But now he realized that companionship with Justine Clemens would never be enough. She made him feel too much. Want too much. Even in the throes of his late-blooming college-hormone explosion, he hadn't been this irresistibly drawn to the woman he eventually married.

And he couldn't give his heart or risk his children's hearts by bringing someone new into their lives. Maybe if the events of the past two years hadn't occurred, he would be able to respond to his feelings for Justine. But all the old trust and control issues he'd thought he'd buried with his father had risen to the surface to haunt him. It was clear from the expression on Justine's face that she couldn't comprehend not trusting God. But then, she was a minister. What had he expected?

And thinking of her career choice brought another possible problem with a relationship to mind. What if Justine's career was more important to her than the girls were? What if a relationship between them didn't work out, but he got his children's hopes up? Gina already wanted a mother fiercely. If he began to date, Gina, at least, would expect a mother to follow.

Besides, he rationalized, he was too wrapped up in caring for the girls to find time for another person in his life. How could he take time for dating without cheating his daughters? Even with Elizabeth Neal's help, it was all he could do to get home from work, handle homework and prepare the two younger girls for bed.

And Justine *was* a minister. As they'd walked out, he'd seen the speculation on the faces of the other patrons at Harry's. Even if she were interested—which, after the whole trust discussion, he doubted—she still had to be extra careful of her reputation or any hint of impropriety. No. This would be the last time he'd ask Justine to meet him for lunch or any other meal.

It had to be.

# Chapter Six

"See, Daddy. I told you all your worrying was silly," Leslie told her father as they left Dr. Whitlark's office. *Silly and embarrassing. Did they all think she was an idiot? That she didn't know exactly what she was doing?*

Leslie hid a smile, knowing right then that it would give away her triumphant feelings. She'd outsmarted all of them. Daddy, Reverend Clemens, Miss Neal and Nurse Gracie Hart. They'd all been watching her. Which was pretty creepy. It was just lucky that she'd gotten so many tricks off that anorexia Internet site or she might have fallen behind on her goal.

The last tip she'd gotten there had been the best yet and a real lifesaver. Drinking all that water in the ladies' room just before the doctor saw her had been a perfect solution to the surprise doctor visit her father had sprung on her last night. Just as promised, water could boost her weight by a pound a pint. Drinking a gallon and a half of water had been really hard, but she'd done it and had kept it down. When she'd stepped on the scale it had looked as if she hadn't lost more than a few measly pounds. And now they'd all get off her back!

Brilliant. She was giddy with relief. And she'd be home free if she could just wait to go to the bathroom till they got to church for rehearsal on the play the kids in the After-School Days program were doing for the Harvest Festival.

"Are you staying to watch us practice?" she asked her dad, beaming him a big smile as they climbed into his car.

"I'd planned on it since Miss Neal said it's a dress rehearsal. I'll be on call tomorrow and might be needed somewhere else in town while the play is going on. You don't mind, do you, princess?"

"It's okay that you need to be on patrol during the festival."

Her father grinned. "I meant my watching tonight. It won't make you or Cindy nervous, will it?"

"Not as long as you sit out front as part of our practice audience. A few of Miss Neal's friends are watching, too. I just don't want you hanging around backstage," she said. She had to make sure her father was out front, where he couldn't monitor her trips to the ladies' room.

Matt felt lighter than air as he watched Leslie tear into the church, eager to see her friends and get ready for the dress rehearsal. Les wasn't the same angry girl today that she'd been for weeks. She'd been annoyed last night about the doctor's appointment, but, by this morning, she'd done an about face and had said it would be nice to see Doc Whitlark again.

Thankfully, Les's pediatrician hadn't seen a problem with her. Everything was fine. In fact, surprisingly, Les had lost only five pounds since her last checkup. Granted, that had been a year ago, but if her doctor thought that was normal for a girl her age, who was Matt to argue. He was just a worried father. Whitlark was a doctor.

Matt closed his eyes and just enjoyed, for a second, the feeling of having nothing to worry about. Now Justine could stop worrying, too, he thought. It had touched him that she said she thought of Les at every meal. He hadn't seen her since their lunch over a week ago, and he couldn't wait to tell her the good news.

Justine wasn't the only one thinking about others at odd times. It happened all the time to him, too. Look at the way she'd just popped into his head. And it usually happened at the strangest and most inconvenient times. The whole town probably thought their new police chief was an idiot by now.

He would walk into Harry's Kitchen and be instantly distracted, his mind off on a tangent about Justine. Invariably someone would strike up a conversation about something happening around town and he'd find himself in the middle of an exchange he knew nothing about.

Or he'd be on the phone, look out his office window and catch sight of First Peninsula's steeple. He'd instantly drift off into thoughts that had nothing to do with the phone conversation and everything to do with one tall, lithe blonde with big brown eyes and a gentle smile. And he'd be left trying to play catch-up on yet another conversation.

But those hours after his kids were tucked in were the worst of the day. The quiet of the house seemed to magnify his isolation. He'd tried reading, folding laundry, channel surfing through two hundred uninteresting programs. Nothing filled the silent solitude of the night anymore.

Last night during that time, he'd finally admitted he was attracted to Justine on more levels than he'd thought. It was more than his physical reaction and the desire she stirred in him. He was sure he'd be able to ignore that aspect of his interest in her, though it was a powerful pull, were it not for the other thing. It was the emotional and spiritual need that really sank his boat. And so he'd realized he would have to find a way to carefully explore his feelings for her. How, he'd yet to work out, especially the way she felt about trusting God.

As Matt walked down the sidewalk toward the front of the church, Kyle and Gracie Hart crossed the street, clearly headed for the church, too. When he and Kyle had come to Safe Harbor, they had had a lot in common. They were the same age, both of them had lost a wife and both had come to Safe Harbor searching for a better, more fulfilling life. Of course, Matt hadn't lost a child as Kyle had. This recent worry over Leslie, though, was an additional parallel between them that was a little too close for comfort.

"Do we have two more recruits for Miss Neal's test audience?" Matt asked Kyle and Gracie as they came even with him on the pavement.

Kyle shook his head and shot Gracie an affectionate look. "I got volunteered."

"Miss Neal needed last minute help for the youth play," Gracie hastened to explain.

Matt checked his watch. "Well, I don't know about you two, but I have to get myself front and center. All three of the girls are in this thing, and I'll lose my membership in the Father of the Year Club if I'm late."

Matt left the couple chuckling as he hurried into the church hall and up to the front row. He was just in time for the curtain to rise. First Cindy, then Gina, appeared on stage acting out their roles in the play about a family of farmers and their trip to the State Fair.

The musical progressed without mistakes or serious incidents until the high-pitched scream of a young girl echoed from back stage. Matt was pretty sure it wasn't part of the State Fair script, and then Elizabeth Neal tore onto the stage.

"Chief Trent! It's Leslie. One of the girls just found her unconscious in the powder room."

Matt was on his feet and running. "Kyle and Gracie are here somewhere," he called across the stage to Miss Neal, and at the same time he heard Constance Laughlin say something about calling 911.

Seeing Justine perform CPR on his child was the last thing he'd expected to find when he got to the old tiled bathroom. As he entered, she was in the process of moving from doing chest compressions to doing mouth-to-mouth resuscitation.

Matt knew CPR, but at that moment he could scarcely draw a breath for himself. Like a statue, he stood staring in frozen horror as Leslie lay lifeless on the floor.

"Matt! Did they call 911?" Justine demanded.

The urgent tone in her voice snapped him into action. "Constance did," he said as he moved into position at Leslie's head.

"Go," Justine ordered. "Two breaths."

Matt would be eternally grateful to her for keeping him on track, because if he thought too deeply about what was happening, he wasn't sure he'd be able to function at all. Then, after several more terrifying moments out of time, Kyle and Gracie rushed in and Justine pulled him aside to make room for the professionals.

"She's in cardiac arrest," Kyle announced calmly. "Reverend, is that defibrillator you were going to get the board to approve on hand yet?"

Matt hadn't even realized Reverend Burns was standing in the doorway until he spoke. "It arrived today," the older man said. "Justine, it's in the left bottom drawer of my desk. You're faster on your feet than I am. I'm going to finish herding all the children into the hall. It looks as if we need to get a dedicated prayer team to work. When Justine suggested we buy that thing I surely never thought it would be a young one who'd use it."

Justine was gone before Reverend Burns finished his scattered thoughts. Then the older man left, shaking his head in wonder, his face creased with worry.

"Matt, is she on any medication?" Kyle asked while Gracie blew breaths into Leslie's lungs.

Matt shook his head.

"Any history of problems with drugs or anything else that would explain an episode like this?"

"No. Les is a great kid. She'd never use drugs."

"But she has been having some problems with eating," Justine put in as she reentered with a black and yellow plastic box that she then handed to Kyle.

Matt glared at her. "We just came from her doctor's office. He said Leslie's weight was fine."

Gracie ripped his daughter's shirt open as Kyle readied the defibrillator. "Then, he's blind," the nurse growled. "I can count her ribs."

"Clear," Kyle shouted, and Matt looked down in time to see his little princess's whole body jerk in response to the electric shock. "Again," Kyle called out, and reapplied the paddles. And once again Leslie's body jerked. But this time Kyle sighed in relief. "Regular sinus rhythm," he said. "Let's get her over to the hospital."

Right on time, the metallic clatter of a gurney resounded in the hallway. Matt watched as the attendants and Kyle and Gracie lifted Les onto the stretcher.

He followed, but felt as if he were looking at the whole scene through a hazy curtain. His precious child had almost died. Might still die. And Justine was there, her hand settling on his arm. He looked down, feeling detached and numb.

"You should probably ride with them," she advised gently. "I don't think you should drive even though it's only a couple blocks. I'll see to the girls."

"Cindy and Gina," he said helplessly. "Her sisters have to know what's happening by now."

"You go with Leslie. Elizabeth and I will take care of the girls."

He could only nod, though he realized she'd said that before. It was as if he were sleepwalking through a waking nightmare. He couldn't lose Leslie. Not his precious child.

Then Kyle grabbed his hand. "Hang in there, Matt. I won't let anything happen to your child."

Matt nodded. Having lost his own wife and child in a car accident two years ago, Kyle understood how helpless he felt. How stricken with fear he was.

"Water? She drank too much water?" Justine asked as she sat down across from Matt at his kitchen table. She'd been able to get both girls to sleep once Matt had called to say Leslie was out of danger, and she'd sent Elizabeth home because the poor dear had worried herself to a frazzle. "How could drinking water nearly kill her?"

"Apparently she read something that said a pint of water weighs a pound." Matt looked at her sadly. "She drank over a gallon of water to boost her weight when I took her to see Dr. Whitlark. Her weight was only a little off what it had been the last time he saw her. He said that wasn't outside the norm for girls her age, and when Les balked at getting undressed for him, he said that isn't unusual, either.

"I noticed her going into the ladies' room at

church several times, but she said she was checking her makeup. Which also isn't odd in a girl her age." But Justine felt she should have known. Les had nearly died.

"Please don't. I hear guilt in your voice," Matt said, his voice low and flat. "It's me who missed all this. You tried to tell me. Kyle says that when she voided all that water, she was already so depleted from not eating, her electrolyte and potassium levels bottomed out and her heart just stopped. He said your quick thinking saved her life. That, along with the defibrillator you talked the board into buying for the church. I don't know how I'll ever repay you."

"There's nothing to repay," Justine said softly, "but you could do something that will help me sleep tonight. Come look at the stuff I found on the Internet. I've also pulled up the Web site for that eating disorder clinic I told you about. There are only a few clinics like it in the country. It's a miracle there's one so close."

"But she learned her lesson."

Justine could see the fear in Matt's face and hear the desperate hope in his voice.

"Please," she said.

Matt sighed and stood. He was really dragging, and she never would have pushed him if a child's life wasn't at stake. He led the way up the stairs to what was clearly a thirteen-year-old's room. There were a myriad of dolls, but they were tucked away on the shelves, showing that Les's childhood might be over but a part of her still secretly mourned the end of it. Justine remembered the feeling all too well.

A computer on a sleek workstation was in the far corner surrounded by bookshelves and discarded running shoes. Matt sat down and booted up the machine. As he dialed up their Internet provider, something Justine had read the week before came to mind.

"Matt, do you often clear out the history file on your Internet browser?

"Confession time. I'm not sure."

"Okay. Drop that box down," she told him, pointing at the screen. "Now that. Now that. There. Those are the sites she's been on in the past ten days."

There it was in glaring black and white: visit after visit to several sites about weight control and anorexia. "So she was worried, too." Matt sighed.

Justine really hated to burst his bubble. "Matt, call up one or two of those Web sites. Check them out," she urged him. "Look at what she's been reading."

Matt glanced over his shoulder at her. He looked as if his heart was breaking. "I feel like I'm spying on her."

Putting a hand on his shoulder, she gave it a reassuring squeeze. "You are. But she isn't making good decisions for herself, so you have to do it for her for a while longer. If it helps you save her life, you've done the right thing.''

"Okay.'' He nodded, pursed his lips and turned back to the PC. The machine chuffed a little, blinked a little. And then the first site popped up. Pictures of perceived but distorted beauty built before them. A fashion model everyone thought was too thin shared center stage with a young girl who looked like a detainee at Auschwitz. The fashion model clearly needed to lose weight, it said.

Matt's hand shook as he scrolled through that site and two more. Further exploration through the computer's memory turned up a copy of a disturbing e-mail. Les must have gone into a support chat room and another unfortunate victim of the insidious disease had sent a private e-mail just last night. It contained advice on the weight of water and the idea that drinking water was a way to disguise weight loss from prying parents and doctors.

Only when he turned toward her did Justine realize her silent vigil at Matt's side was over. "Matt, you couldn't have known she—''

"No. Don't! There's absolutely nothing you can say that will make me feel better. Nor should I. I've been an absolute idiot.''

Still facing him and not breaking eye contact, Justine sank to the edge of the window seat next to the computer desk, willing him to listen. "First, you can't crucify yourself for believing in your child. All parents want to do that. Now, having said that, I'm here to listen to whatever you have to say.''

"I was wrong. About Les. But mostly about God. He knew she was up to all this but I didn't go to Him with my worry. I think I've just wanted someone convenient to blame for the disappointments and losses in my life.''

"I'd bet He knows that. I'm not saying it didn't hurt Him, but He's very quick to forgive. It isn't even as if you turned your back on Him. You made sure your girls knew Him. You worship Him openly.''

"Yeah, but I kept Him in a little box labeled 'Sunday' and 'Behavior Code.' Cindy told me about the homily you gave last week at the kids' midweek service. I did what you warned them about. I put Him where He couldn't do a lot of good in our lives.''

She felt as if she were witnessing a miracle. Matt had learned a lot in a few short minutes. "Yes, you did. But it isn't too late to fix things.''

"You asked what you could do. You could pray with me,'' he said, extending his hand toward her.

Justine hesitated. Not because she was reluctant to pray with him but because his touch did crazy things to her. However, he needed her support and she couldn't withhold it. She quickly decided what she would do was to steer him to Reverend Burns for spiritual counseling at the first opportunity. Holding her breath, Justine took his hand and studiously ignored the frisson that skittered through her.

"Father," she prayed, "I ask you to hear your servant Matt and to comfort him in this time of fear, worry and disappointment over his child. I ask You to guide the decisions he must make for his daughter's welfare. And I ask a special blessing on Leslie, a good and sweet child, who has put her foot on a wrong and dangerous path. Guide us in helping You heal her life and her soul."

"Lord—" Matt said, his voice breaking after a few moments of reflective silence. "I've been a real idiot and I'm sorry. I've been so intent on holding my children close that I endangered one of them, thinking I could protect them better than anyone. Including You. I was even warned she had a problem but I didn't listen. Maybe it was pride. I sure hope not. Mostly, I think it was fear. I guess I thought if I denied it, the problem just wouldn't exist.

"This stuff I found on the computer tonight and what she did to hide the truth this afternoon sort of proves this is bigger and more complicated than I can deal with on my own. And that I shouldn't have tried. I need Your help, Your guidance, as Justine said. I'm so sorry I didn't turn to You—" Matt whispered, his voice breaking again. He took a deep breath. "Please, tell me what to do."

He looked up, blinking back tears. "Now what?"

Justine took a deep breath, willing her tears back. "Well, we came up here to check out the Internet for help, but I sidetracked us. Suppose we look for guidance out there. When I went looking before, I put in 'anorexia' as a search word and pages of sites came up."

Matt nodded and turned back to the computer. Though he used a different search engine than she had, the screen soon displayed an extensive list. Matt picked one site at random, and Justine, though a strong believer in trusting God, blinked in disbelief as the site built. It was the one for the Mittler Center—the clinic in Green Bay she'd spoken to.

Matt's grin was tinged with sadness. "I guess He listened."

She swallowed deeply. "I would have to say, He also answered."

"When they release her from the hospital, I'll have to take her there, won't I?" Again he was blinking back tears.

It was hard for Justine not to give in to the urge to hold him and cry with him. But she had to remain strong, and knew he did, too. "If they have room, I'd say that would be best. I think that's what God's saying to you right now. I'm just not equipped to help her, Matt. I'll talk to the people at the center again. See if they still have a place for her. I'll also see her as often as I'm allowed so I can add a Godly perspective on what she'll be taught. But understand, they have a much better idea of what's going on in her head than anyone else because they deal with this every day.''

Matt nodded. ''Thanks. What they'll tell her about moral and spiritual issues worries me a little.''

''I checked that out before I mentioned them to you. They make it a policy to never circumvent the religious belief structure of the patients.'' She hesitated to hand him anything else to deal with that night, but one more thing did have to be addressed. ''And, Matt, don't count on her being happy about the center.''

''You think she'll fight me.'' It wasn't a question.

''Oh, yes. She's put a great deal of energy into fooling you and herself that there's nothing wrong with what she's been doing. That won't change overnight. Even if she sees that it's dangerous, she isn't going to be able to give up the control that not eating has given her. Any more than it's going to be easy for you to give control over her and your life to God. I think you might find it helpful to talk to Reverend Burns often in the next several weeks.''

''Not you?''

Justine shook her head. ''Reverend Burns is your spiritual adviser, Matt.''

She hoped he wouldn't ask why she couldn't work with him. Could she admit to her feelings for him? Explain that it would be improper for her to advise him when she couldn't be impartial or detached? She could but preferred not to, since she could do nothing about her feelings for him.

Thankfully, he didn't question her further, asking instead, "Will you come with me when I take her to this Mittler Center? As a…friend?"

"I'll be glad to," she said, smiling but feeling an annoying disappointment that he saw her as a friend. Talk about a dog in the manger….

Matt nodded and turned back to the computer. He shut it down and unplugged it. "Mind giving me a hand with this? I'm going to move it to the family room. I should never have given in when Leslie begged to have it in her room. She said the other two distracted her when she was doing her homework. And Cindy and Gina have less homework and want to watch TV before bed, so the family room just didn't work. When Les comes home, we'll have to work out an answer to the problem, but having it up here was a bad idea. I want it where I can monitor what they're exposed to."

"How about putting it in that corner of the eating area of the kitchen? If you take the leaf out of the table, it'll fit just fine. You can make the kitchen 'homework central.'"

"Hmm. I thought you were terrible with space

and home decoration. Could it be you told a little white lie to boost my daughter's self-esteem?''

Justine blushed a becoming color of pink and picked up the monitor he'd just disconnected. ''I'm pleading the Fifth.''

''What a cop-out,'' Matt accused, following her with the PC tower and keyboard under his arm.

''Exactly!'' she called over her shoulder. ''Do you want me to help you bring down the rest?'' she asked as she set the monitor down on the kitchen table.

''Naw. You go home and get some sleep. Somehow I don't see myself closing my eyes tonight. This'll give me something to do.'' He hadn't realized he'd gotten so close to her until she turned and looked up at him. Her eyes were gentle and kind. He thought he could fall into them and be completely at peace. It wasn't the usual feeling she inspired. Strange that she affected him on so many levels.

''Okay. Home it is. You'll call if I can do anything?''

''I'll talk to the people at the Mittler Center and be in touch when I find out she's going to be released from the hospital. Thanks,'' he said, barely recognizing his own voice.

Justine was right to hand him off to Reverend Burns. The way he felt about her would make asking her advice on spiritual matters a mistake. Because to him, she was more a warm and desirable woman than she was a minister—and always would be.

# *Chapter Seven*

"Daddy, please," Leslie begged. "Don't leave me here. I'll miss you so much. Gina and Cindy need me."

Matt glanced over Leslie's head at Justine, trying to draw from her quiet strength. Leslie had been so cooperative thus far that he'd fooled himself into believing they would be spared this scene.

The three of them had toured the terrific old estate. The main house, which was really a huge mansion converted for its current purpose, had beautifully appointed public rooms. Even more impressive were the private residential suites for the patients—mostly young women in their teens and early twenties.

While Leslie was evaluated by Dr. Sheila Kiley, he and Justine met Samantha Mittler. A dynamo of a senior citizen, she still maintained her golden-blond hair and youthful glow. Justine asked what had lead her family to endow the center.

Pain had entered Mrs. Mittler's pale blue eyes. "My husband and I were blessed with money, position and a terrifically happy life. Mostly we were blessed with a daughter who was as bright and beautiful as any star in the sky. One day I noticed she'd begun to get a little too thin. 'Thin is in, Mom,' she told me. I nodded and said, 'But not too thin,' and went on my happy way. Months later I walked in on her when she was dressing and was appalled at what I saw. I took her to the doctor, sure she had some terrible wasting disease. She did, but not one I'd ever heard of. No one knew what to do for her. How to get through to her. She died two years later of a heart attack brought on by anorexia nervosa. That was the eighties when the disease was little known or understood. This," she said gesturing at the stately home around them, "was our answer. We wanted other children to have a chance. Other parents to be spared our pain. It is all that kept us going."

She went on to explain that the mansion had been their home, that after their daughter's death she and her late husband had poured their lives and fortune into the Mittler Center. Out of the pain of loss they'd found a mission. The couple had moved into a small groundskeeper's cottage, where Samantha still lived, and had turned their family estate into a center of healing and hope, a facility to battle an unseen enemy.

The condition of many of the other residents was a real wake-up call to Matt, though he no longer needed one. This disease was a killer and it worked slowly, insidiously, turning victims into shadows of what God had intended them to be.

The Mittler Center was a bright and beautiful place. More important, it was a progressive facility where the patients were treated in ways never before considered. Next they met Dr. Sheila Kiley, who had brilliant green eyes and strawberry-blond hair. Dr. Kiley was the head psychiatrist. It fell to her to explain Leslie's treatment.

"Please come in. I've spoken to Leslie at length. She doesn't exactly confirm all you told me on the phone, but enough of it that I feel our residential program would be advantageous for her. In fact, I think it imperative that she stay with us. She feels otherwise, but I hope you'll consider it seriously. She's a little younger than our average resident, but there are other teens here."

Justine watched as Matt struggled with the thought of leaving his daughter behind. "What kind of treatment would she require? You said it's different for everyone."

"Leslie will enter a four-stage program. The first concentrates on safety. We'll work to eliminate the immediate danger presented by the disorder.

"The second stage will help develop coping

skills so she can confront and understand the underlying cause of her problem. The center treats anorexia, bulimia and compulsive overeating. Leslie is anorexic.

"The next stage will move her into a relapse prevention phase. Its aim is to help her develop a healthy relationship with food and will hopefully arm her with coping skills so she can maintain emotional health once she leaves.

"The last was designed to ease the patient back into a routine lifestyle with the confidence to maintain a healthy eating pattern. At that point Leslie would probably begin attending a private school near here, then return in the afternoons to the center, where she could still participate in evening programs."

Next they'd talked to a couple of young graduates of the program who now worked as counselors. Seeing those two lovely women healthy and well-adjusted gave Matt hope for Leslie. He knew the Mittler Center was the right move for his daughter, but that didn't make leaving her there any easier.

Leslie had apparently seen through his positive comments. Justine had warned him that Les would try to play on his worry, but he'd hoped she had accepted the rightness of the center for her. Then had come the time to say goodbye.

After she began begging him to reconsider his decision to have her admitted and trying to sound positive and supportive, Matt took her by the shoulders and said, ''I have to leave you here. And Cindy and Gina want you healthy so you'll always be around to be a big sister to them. This is a really nice place. Think of taking long walks in those gardens. You've always loved nature trails.''

She pulled away and hugged herself. ''It's a prison. I can't do this. Please don't leave me here.'' Her voice became a sob. ''Don't desert me.''

''I'm not deserting you, princess.'' Matt struggled to keep his voice strong yet compassionate. ''I'm putting you in the hands of people who can help you. They *can* help you. I can't. And you'll meet other patients who are struggling with the same problem you are.''

''I don't *have* a problem. Not anymore. I'm not stupid. I almost died. I won't do anything like that again.''

Matt sighed. She still didn't see her real problem. How, he couldn't imagine. But it was clear the Mittler Center was exactly what she needed. ''Drinking all that water to boost your weight was a symptom, not the problem. The weight loss. The cardiac arrest. Those are still symptoms. Your problem is thinking you *needed* to stop eating. We eat to live, princess. Our bodies need fuel to burn or they shut off. Last night yours did just that!''

''Okay. I get it!'' she shouted.

She was getting angry, and Matt thanked God for it. Angry he could deal with. Pathetic pleas and helpless looks? He wasn't so sure. She was his little girl, after all. He shot her the steely-eyed look he'd been practicing and using on her for years whenever she stepped over the line.

"Don't shout at me, young lady. I brought you here so you can get your head straight. You can't convince me you don't need to be here. The professionals working here are the only ones who will tell me you're ready to come home. Right now, they all agree you need this place."

"Why are you doing this to me?" Leslie yelled at him. "If you don't want me, send me to live with Gran. Gran wouldn't do this to me. She wanted me to live with her. I hate you! If you leave me here, I'll hate you forever."

"You could have died last night!" Matt shouted back. Taking a heaving breath he tried to steady his voice. "I'm doing this because I love you. Someday maybe you'll believe that. The truth is, there's nothing you can say to me to change my mind because I'd rather have you live to hate me than die loving me. I'll see you soon, princess. I love you. Try not to hate me. It'll only hurt both of us."

He turned and all but ran out of her room and down a nearby set of stairs.

"Daddy, please!"

Matt heard Leslie scream but he didn't stop. Nor did he look to see if Justine had followed or if he'd left her behind to clean up after his cowardly retreat. He moved forward, knowing he would forever hear his child's broken voice calling to him as he fled. He'd forever have to face the fact that he'd turned his back and walked away, leaving her in the care of strangers.

Matt didn't even see the gorgeous gardens as he headed to his car. He climbed behind the wheel and sat staring into space, his head pressed to the headrest and his hands gripping the wheel. He had no idea how long he sat there like a broken robot, unable to move with his splintered memory replaying the scene and torturing him with the sound of her last agonized cry.

He didn't notice Justine return to the car or even know how long she'd been there when the balm of her silent understanding finally penetrated his private agony. It sent his defenses tumbling. Tears burned his throat as they pressed to escape. He blinked but it was no use. One after another the tears broke free and rolled down his cheeks. He shook his head to wrestle back control, but then Justine touched his shoulder. That tipped the scales.

Matt gave up and curled forward against the wheel, abandoning all thoughts of fighting the emotions he'd always hidden from the women in his life. Justine was strong enough to lean on, but compassionate, too. Instinctively he knew she wouldn't think less of him because his child could break his heart.

It was as if a storm had built up inside a box and now the lid had been torn off. He somehow managed to keep from sobbing openly, but couldn't stem the tide of his tears or keep his shoulders from shaking.

"If only she didn't hate me," he whispered when most of the storm had passed.

"Oh, Matt," Justine said. "She doesn't hate you. She's afraid and looking for someone or something to lash out at. You're the perfect target right now because she knows you'll love her no matter what. After you left she said this is the first time in her life she's been away from family. We've cut her off from her world. All her safety lines are gone. She's being forced to confront her problem head-on. And it's a huge problem. That would be frightening even for an adult."

"It isn't just what she said. It's that I couldn't just make it better. I could always make it better before. Not when Diane died, of course. But, even then, after seeing their mother fade away in pain day after day, they just wanted to know she was in a better place. They were remarkably okay with it. All they wanted was for everything else to stay the way it was. I managed to give them that for as long as it still seemed to matter."

Matt wiped his eyes with the back of his hand and stared out the window. "At least, I thought I had. Now, it looks as if I was wrong to bring them here. Les didn't have this problem in Green Bay."

"Weren't you listening to Samantha Mittler?" Justine asked quietly. "This would have happened somewhere down the line for another reason if it hadn't happened now. With her daughter, it was starting college. That far in the future, like them, you might not have noticed. The pattern would have become more ingrained and harder to break. Permanent damage could have been done."

"But—"

"But nothing." Justine's voice became firm and strong. "I have no doubt that every decision you've made since that child was born was in the best interest of her and later in your other children's best interests. It's who you are."

Matt thought about that and had to admit it was true. His kids were his priority and always had been. When Di was alive, they were her priority, too. They'd been more partners in parenthood and friends than lovers. Even during their courtship they'd been friends planning to have children. And they had worked their lives around their daughters.

Matt nodded, accepting Justine's opinion as truth. The move to Safe Harbor had been good for Cindy and Gina, and eventually would be good for Les, too. He looked over at Justine. Concern and that quiet serenity of hers glowed from her lovely dark eyes, and he felt a strange jolt.

Maybe he needed to think a little harder about

being more than just a father. Maybe the move to
Safe Harbor would turn out to be a good thing for
him, as well.

As they left the grounds, Justine watched Matt
look over his shoulder, back up the long tree-lined
drive at the Mittler Center. Her heart simply ached
for him. She didn't think it was too far-fetched to
assume he'd seen Leslie every day of her life. It
wouldn't be easy to deal with her being gone, or
to explain her continued absence to Cindy and
Gina. Nor would it be easy tonight, when Matt had
to walk past Leslie's empty room on the way to
his own, knowing it would be dark and empty for
some time to come. Justine couldn't help with that,
but she could help with the girls. She was, after
all, the girls' pastor.

"Would it help if I explained Leslie's hospital-
ization to Cindy and Gina?"

"You have no idea how much. I don't know
how I'm going to get through that right now. But
I took the coward's way out this morning. I let
them sleep and left as soon as Miss Neal arrived.
The news should come from me."

"You are so hard on yourself, Matthew Trent.
Those children needed their sleep this morning.
Goodness, it had to be almost midnight by the time
Elizabeth and I got them settled down and asleep
last night. And you had Leslie to think of and all
the arrangements to make with the Mittler Center."

She hoped she could brighten his spirits, if not

for his sake then for his children's. They were sure to sense his unsettled mood. "Elizabeth is more than up to the task of distracting them. She already expected to have them with her today. By the time they fell asleep, they were both excited and looking forward to being her assistants today. I think they see themselves stepping directly into her shoes when she gives up running the Harvest Festival. They'll be having a ball and not thinking about you or Leslie all day."

"You think?"

She had to smile at his hopeful tone and the look in his dark eyes when he glanced over at her. "I *know*. I also know the news would seem less serious coming from me. They'll see your unsettled feelings if you try to tell them. Let me do this for the three of you."

Matt nodded his agreement, but not without a little grimace that she knew meant he still thought himself cowardly for letting her handle his problem.

"Thank you for your trust. Now let's get home. I don't work the ice-cream concession till three-thirty, but we have to be there by one for the musical and to give me time to talk to Cindy and Gina."

It was nearly four when Matt and the girls showed up at the ice-cream concession stand. They had changed out of their costumes and were bouncing with anticipation. The smell of popcorn wafted through the grounds on the crisp fall air, and riding along with it were a myriad of tunes and the distant sound of the game barkers.

And it was all out there waiting. Excitement. The kind that only this kind of day could bring to the faces of children. You could read it in the sparkle in the girl's eyes and see it in the spring in their steps. The sky was bright, promising a clear evening ahead. Soon the midway would be lit by hundreds of lights, and brilliant neon strips would illuminate the rides.

Cindy and Gina had taken news of Leslie's stay at the center surprisingly well. All they'd wanted was an assurance of her eventual return home. After they had that, and with all the surprising resilience of youth, they'd gone on to perform in the play. Gina's performance, while not as flawless as Cindy's, was certainly memorable for its originality.

"What can I get for these two lovely ladies and their handsome father?" Justine asked as they stepped up to the booth.

"Ice cream," the girls chorused.

"Vanilla cones and lots of napkins," Matt added, grinning down at the duo.

"Here you go," Justine said as she handed each girl the swirled soft-serve. "Compliments of the house to the stars of today's play. You were both wonderful."

"It's not fair Leslie had to miss it," Cindy grumbled.

"I noticed that nice Mr. Taylor making a video of the play," Justine said quickly. "I asked if I could have a copy. I thought when I visit Leslie in a couple weeks, I'd take it along. She can play it for everyone staying at the center."

"Do you think she's sad she missed it?" Gina asked. "She helped us learn our parts."

"I'm sure she was sad to miss it, but she needs to be where she is right now. We talked about that. Remember?" Both girls nodded. "Good. And I'm just as sure that seeing how well you both did will make her feel very proud."

"There's that nasty Alan Tobridge," Cindy said.

"Oh, dear," she muttered, noting he seemed to be moving in their direction. "How is he doing?" Justine asked Matt, hoping to distract him.

"So far, so good. He shows up on time and he hasn't given anyone any trouble that I've heard about."

Justine was surprised to see that Alan, his eyes apparently centered on Matt, continued to walk toward the concession stand rather than turn and head the other way. And he wasn't walking with the regular slouching gate he used like a shield whenever she saw him around town. There was purpose to his stride, though it was tinged with reluctance. Matt raised an eyebrow, silently telling her he was just as surprised as she was at this turn of events.

"Chief, my sister told me about…uh…about your kid, uh…Leslie. I wanted to say I'm sorry." The boy's voice shook.

Matt's eyebrows drew together. He was clearly perplexed by Alan's obvious emotional turmoil. She and Matt had talked on the way home from Green Bay about his conversation with Alan over his behavior toward Leslie, Cindy and Gina.

"Thanks, Alan," Matt said, real gratitude in his tone.

If he'd been trying to increase Alan's sense of guilt, it seemed to work.

"No. You don't get it. It's my fault. It's *all* my fault. I never meant to hurt her," Alan went on, staring at the ground. "I mean… I guess I did but… See, I was mad that you were on to me and catching me at everything I did. I thought I'd tease her and she'd go running to you and you'd…you know…be bugged like you were. But I didn't think she'd believe me and, like, starve herself just because I called her fat." The boy's face crumpled.

"Monica says I did this to her. She says Leslie almost died because of me and my big mouth. I swear I didn't mean for her to take me so seriously. She's pretty and smart. I never thought she'd be anything but mad."

Matt checked his watch. "Justine, could you

keep an eye on Cindy and Gina for a little while. I think I'd better have a private talk with Alan.''

Justine pulled the hinged section of the counter up and motioned the girls in. She watched Matt and Alan walk off, silently praying this was the breakthrough with the teen they'd hoped for. She knew Matt. He would insist Alan make some kind of reparation to Leslie. Personal reparation. It would enforce lessons learned but also provide the troubled boy some much-needed relief from the strain of guilt.

It also gave Justine the opportunity to turn the event into a lesson for Matt's younger daughters.

''Girls, do you know what forgiveness is?''

# Chapter Eight

"Cindy's such a daredevil," Matt said, looking up at the ride ahead on the midway. "Are you sure you don't mind waiting with Gina?" he asked for about the tenth time, standing next to the tenth ride they'd come to. Justine really wanted to say, yes, she minded a lot, but there was her image to consider.

She glanced up at the Octopus, her all-time favorite ride, and down at her flowing calf-length skirt. She hadn't been on one of those crazy things in years and she simply itched for the dizzying weightless experience. But not in this skirt. And not in the town whose respect she was trying so hard to earn.

Doubts niggled at her. She looked around, wondering if by pretending to be staid and sober, she wasn't cheating her congregation as much as she was cheating herself. She noticed Constance Laughlin and Nathan Taylor climb onto the next ride over. The Tilt-A-Whirl started up, and Justine couldn't take her eyes off the older couple as gravity slid Constance into Nathan's arms.

She imagined herself sliding into Matt's waiting embrace. A little twinge in the vicinity of her heart made her turn to Matt with a false smile plastered on her face. "Why would I mind spending my time with such an interesting conversationalist?"

Matt's brow crinkled as he raised a skeptical eyebrow. But then he shot that teasing grin at her. "Overplayed, Rev. This is the last ride for a while. I promise. After this, we'll go try our luck at a few games of chance and get over to see that Kit Peters exhibition that the Women's League set up. Not that I know art from a hill of beans, but I'll bet you ladies will enjoy it."

He playfully tossed Cindy over his shoulder as she protested her interest in looking at a bunch of dumb pictures. Laughing, Matt ran off toward the line in front of Justine's beloved Octopus, leaving her staring openmouthed after him.

*Rev?* How irreverent was that? And why did its very irreverence make her want to smile?

"Justine," Constance called to her as she and Nathan strode off the ride a few minutes later. "Isn't this marvelous!"

Curious, Justine thought. According to Elizabeth, nothing about the festival looked one bit different this year from last. Not even the color of the booths had changed. Justine smiled, wondering if perhaps it was the company Constance was keeping lately. She also wondered if Constance knew what a dead giveaway her delight was. Whatever the reason, though, it was nice to see her so happy.

Constance had gone out of her way to make Justine welcome when she'd returned to help Reverend Burns, by inviting her to join the Safe Harbor Women's League. But gratitude not withstanding, from what Justine understood, the past several years had been difficult for Constance. Her husband had taken time off from his career to travel to Central America on a missionary trip with men from his home church. While there building homes for the poor, Joseph Laughlin was killed in some sort of raid on the village.

Constance had weathered the storm beautifully. Instead of becoming bitter, she'd turned her thoughts outward and started the Women's League in the hope of aiding other women facing difficult times. A sizable nest egg allowed her to do all sorts of volunteer work around town as a member of the Safe Harbor Lighthouse Foundation in lieu of building a career.

If anyone deserved a little happiness, it was Constance Laughlin. And who better to find it with than a nice man like Nathan Taylor, the very man who'd rescued her grandson a few months earlier, after he'd been stung by a wasp. Talk about a match made in heaven.

"Harvest Fest is so much more than I remember it being," Justine agreed, fighting a chuckle.

"The improvements are all Elizabeth's doing. It's got a lot to do with her if-a-job's-worth-doing-it's-worth-doing-right philosophy," Constance said. "She's the one who talked the Women's League into taking Harvest Fest over from the chamber of commerce a year after the league started meeting. Then she took charge and off it went."

Gina tugged at the sleeve of Justine's sweater. "Can you go on the merry-go-round with me? It makes Daddy sick."

Justine looked ahead at Matt and Cindy standing in line. "Are you sure? He's ridden every ride."

Gina shrugged.

Constance glanced at Nathan, and he nodded almost imperceptibly, his midnight-dark eyes, usually expressionless, sparkling in the clear fall sunlight. "You know what, Gina, we were just going that way. How would you like to come with us? I just love that carousel. It's a double-decker! I have a feeling Reverend Clemens would really like to ride that big scary Octopus. If you ride the carousel with me, she can go ride with your daddy and big sister. *And* you'll give us an excuse to take a turn on my favorite ride."

"Nuh-unh," Gina said, shaking her head, her

dark curls bobbing in the breeze. She raised her tiny pointed chin stubbornly. "Reverend Clemens doesn't like big scary rides, just like I don't."

Constance grinned. "Oh, I'd bet she does. I'd bet it's her deep dark secret."

Justine blinked. How would Constance know that? "I promised Matt I'd wait here with Gina," Justine countered. "I couldn't just transfer her to someone else's care. It wouldn't be right. Not without his—"

"Then we'll go ask him," Constance put in. "Let's go, Nathan." Suddenly Justine was standing alone, watching the couple walk toward Matt and Cindy, Gina happily swinging between them. Their three dark heads were bobbing as they romped away from her.

Justine blinked again and then rushed to keep up with them. The crowd, though, seemed to swell in front of her and keep her from arriving in time to halt the runaway train Constance had become before Justine's very eyes. Apparently, everyone had to be having fun if Constance was.

"Why didn't you say you love amusement rides?" Matt asked. "I thought you were afraid of them and using Gina as an excuse. Here. Get in line with us. Thanks for taking Gina on the merry-go-round," he told Constance and Nathan, without giving Justine a second to protest.

"It's our pleasure," Constance replied, before

Justine could get her tongue untied. "It reminds me of the days when my own were this small."

Nathan shifted restlessly. "We'd better be off before we miss the next turn," he said, then turned toward her. "Reverend Clemens, I'll drop that video of the musical off at the church later in the week. Your girls did the town proud, Chief. Sorry to hear about your oldest. I pray she's better soon."

And then they were gone and the line for the Octopus was moving forward. Before she knew it, Justine found herself buckled into the seat next to Matt. He'd put Cindy on her right so that when the ride started she wouldn't be squashed by both their weights as the centrifugal force built. It was a good plan for Cindy, but not so good for Justine.

It wasn't long before an annoying rule of physics pressed Cindy against Justine, and Justine toward Matt. No matter how hard she tried to hang on to the bar, she slid inexorably closer to him. Her hip touched his, and she realized how ridiculous she looked hanging on to the bar, her spine contorted like a pretzel.

With a sigh, Justine gave up the fight, and, as she did, Matt raised his arm and wrapped it around both her and Cindy. Her tempting vision as she'd watched Nathan and Constance laughing on the Tilt-A-Whirl had come true.

Embarrassed now that she was plastered against him, Justine peeked at Matt's face. He grinned down at her, and his dark eyes seemed to glitter. The grin was three parts mischief, one part something she couldn't name.

Embarrassment fled as her stomach did a somersault that had nothing to do with the ride.

Matt smiled down at Justine. He wasn't sure what he was doing, flirting openly with a minister from his church, especially with his daughter there. He only knew it felt right. He'd come a long way from the night he'd decided that pursuing Justine was a bad idea. Still, he hadn't exactly figured out what to do with all the feelings she evoked in him. The only thing he *had* decided was that he couldn't ignore those feelings forever. With her so close, he had to admit, he didn't have long to make a decision. Because he was going to kiss her soon and the decision would then be out of his hands. She would know how he felt.

But maybe that was exactly what God intended.

After the ride they reclaimed Gina and decided to head for the midway. The festival grounds occupied the green space behind the courthouse, police station and the church. The main entrance to the festival, where the Safe Harbor Women's League had its booths set up, was off Market Square. The carnival rides were set up along Lake Drive.

At the target range, Matt won both girls a stuffed animal, once he figured out how to compensate for the typical off-center carnival gun sight. As he handed Gina her new stuffed horse, he noticed the direction of Justine's gaze and the sweet smile on her lips. The cause wasn't Gina's and Cindy's obvious delight in their new toys, but a huge tan bear dressed in a glossy yellow nor'easter and galoshes.

"Cute," he said next to her ear.

"Especially the pipe. He's so ridiculous. Sort of a Great Lakes version of Paddington. He reminds me of my grandfather for some weird reason. Maybe because Poppy was a commercial fisherman, too. He died a year or so after my father disappeared, so I don't remember much about him except he always smelled like Ivory soap and cherry pipe tobacco."

"How many targets do I have to hit to win that bear?" Matt called to the booth attendant.

"You already won two prizes, buddy," the carnie groused.

"How many targets?" Matt asked again, not to be swayed.

Justine put a hand on his forearm. "Matt, it's okay. I'm a grown woman. I don't need a stuffed bear."

"That's the point of stuffed animals, according to Leslie. You don't need them. But you want them, anyway. And you want him. I see it in your eyes."

The concession operator named a significant number of targets he'd need to hit and grudgingly held out a rifle. Mr. Bear wouldn't come cheaply or easily, but the guy's attitude bugged Matt, so he tossed down a ten-dollar bill and turned to pick up the same rifle he'd been using, ignoring the weapon the operator held. "That's okay. I have this puppy all warmed up."

Ten minutes later Matt laid down the weapon. "And that's that," he said, grinning in triumph at the annoyed operator. Applause rang out from a crowd Matt hadn't realized he'd drawn with his little contest of wills. Several men shouted congratulations, mentioning his position on the force.

A deeper frown creased the face of the guy in the booth. "Hey, you're a ringer. You didn't say you were a cop," he complained.

Matt leaned close. "I didn't mention my sharpshooter status with the FBI, either. But then, you don't warn the nice folks that the sights are purposely machined a little off on all your rifles. The bear for the lady or I just might make a general announcement."

It took no time at all for him to decide to hand the silly bear over to Justine. She blushed and looked utterly charming as she hugged the huge bear in the yellow plastic raincoat and hat.

As they walked away, he noticed Alex Wilkins with his new sons, Connor and Aidan. The twin boys were pointing out the toys they wanted their father to win for them. Matt couldn't resist. He leaned close to Alex's ear. "Go with the third one on the left. Aim low and outside."

Alex grinned. "I owe you one."

"What's his name?" Gina was demanding of Justine when Matt turned back to them.

"Hmm. I'm not sure." Justine held him away from her. "What does he look like to you?" she asked him.

Matt shrugged. "A bear?"

"Daddy! We have to name him," Cindy shouted, and giggled at the same time. It was a magical sound.

"Oh," he said with mock surprise. "Well, Rev, how about Poppy, since he reminded you of your grandfather?"

"Poppy. That's perfect! Poppy the Fisherbear, meet Gina, Cindy and Matthew Trent. It was Matt who freed you from the clutches of that evil game operator back there."

Matt stepped back a little and watched Justine interact with Cindy and Gina. She was a natural at mothering—and wasn't that dangerous territory to tread on so soon? He stopped his instinctive retreat. No, he was trusting God now, and if Justine was supposed to be a part of his life and that of his kids, it would happen. And he would let it happen.

It was up to God to sort out any problems that cropped up along the way.

"Daddy? Can we?"

Shaking himself out of his resolutions and

dreams for the future, Matt looked around for a hint of what the new conversation he'd undoubtedly missed was about. Getting no immediate clue from the festival crowd around them, he asked, "Can you…?"

Justine came to his rescue right on cue. They really were a good team. "Can they try the kids' games the Women's League is running? And over that way I need to stop and place a bid on a quilt I've wanted from the moment I saw it."

It took another hour to get to the quilt booth. The sky had grown dark by then and the grounds were alight with luminous color. Cindy and Gina had cost him ten times the value of the prizes they'd won. But they'd had a ball—and wasn't that the point?

They'd just dropped the girls off at a children's event designed to give parents and their wallets a break, so he was alone with Justine at last. Alone with her and the rest of the adults in town.

But even with all the noisy chatter in the vicinity of the Women's League quilt booth, Matt knew he'd heard right. Justine had just put in a bid of fifty dollars on the worst-looking quilt he'd ever seen. Not that he was an expert, but he had eyes and that was all it took!

"You're kidding, right? It's not even."

"Even what?" she asked, her eyes twinkling.

"Even anything. The seams are crooked and

lumpy. Which I might add seems to be the case with the stuffing, too. And the thing is badly out of square.'' He tilted his head a bit to one side, then the other. ''Is there even a pattern to it? Even I know there's supposed to be a pattern. There's no pattern. It also looks like it won't survive its first good washing.''

''Think so? Well, I like its homemade…uh… frontier quality.''

Matt laughed. ''Frontier quality. It has that. It looks like it was made by a ham-handed, blind cowboy.''

''Humph,'' Justine said, and crossed her arms. She looked back at the quilt. Matt was sure she was trying to look stubborn but there was something too close to amusement in her eyes to let her pull it off. ''I'll have you know,'' she went on, still looking away, ''I've always wanted a picnic quilt. This should fit the bill perfectly. Let me know if I win, Wendy.''

Wendy, looking happy and healthy after the birth of their third child, grinned and shot Justine an incredulous look. ''If?''

''Oh, stop that. I'll drop by at the end of the night to pay up. *If* I win,'' she added after a significant pause. Wendy didn't look a bit less amused as she bid them a cheery goodbye.

They'd almost gotten to Kit's art show when it hit him. Matt grabbed Justine's hand and stopped her in the midst of the flowing crowd. ''Elizabeth made that quilt, didn't she? You warned me about her sewing. And she's a member of the league.''

Justine grinned. ''Can't put one over on you, Chief Trent. It's nice to see the town is safe from all manner of con artists with you on duty.''

He chuckled. ''Yep.'' He tapped his temple. ''A mind like a steel trap. That was a really nice thing you did. Elizabeth's quilt would have sat there gathering dust.''

''We don't know that,'' she hedged. ''I could even lose to someone else who is able to see her vision.''

''Vision? Oh, the frontier look you mentioned. Sure. What do you say we christen it tomorrow after church? I'd like to plan a pretty full day again tomorrow to keep the little ones busy. Hiking in the park and having a picnic lunch is one of their favorite things to do. I'll pack the sandwiches.''

''Tell you what,'' she said, and her smile told him she wasn't going to turn him down. ''Since I *might* be bringing the blanket, I'll bring the lunch we're supposed to eat on it.''

''That hardly seems fair. There are three of us and only one of you.''

''Exactly. Have you any idea how sick I get of cooking for one person? This is a golden opportunity for me. Is there anything the girls especially like?''

His kids had never been fussy. In fact, they were

just the opposite. "With my kids? Whatever isn't nailed down would be a safe bet."

Then suddenly, talk of eating habits had Leslie's plight rushing across the landscape of his mind. All the fear and uncertainty returned. Before him, like a river of pain he knew he'd have to ford, lay the whole perplexing problem, and his spirits took a nose dive.

His child was afraid of food. Of so losing control of her life that she felt she had to control her eating to the point of starvation and near death. What had gone wrong? How could he fix it?

Leslie hadn't been far from his thoughts all along, but as he'd concentrated on making sure Cindy and Gina got through the day, he had, as well. And for a few minutes, every so often, he'd forgotten his own child had technically died the night before.

"Matt, you're white as a ghost. Come on," Justine was saying as she took his arm and literally lead him out of the festival grounds and across the street.

He just couldn't seem to gain his emotional equilibrium. His child was locked away, an hour from home, in what amounted to a psychiatric institution. Her ailment caused an alarming percentage of deaths among sufferers. And today life had gone on without her. Just as it had gone on without her mother. What if it had to go on just as permanently without Les? What if she didn't turn out to be one of the lucky ones?

They entered Market Square, which was surprisingly quiet but for a few people calmly strolling along the footpaths in subdued conversation. Most of the town's residents and tourists appeared to be on the fairgrounds having the time of their lives.

Feeling as if the underpinnings of his whole world had been shaken anew, Matt sank onto a bench and braced his forearms on his knees. Justine turned toward him on the bench, her hand on his shoulder.

"What happened back there?" she asked him gently.

"I remembered last night. Seeing her all but dead. I remembered how still she was while we were trying to breathe life back into her. She can still die of this. All night, that one thought kept me awake, haunting me. All day, I never forgot where she is right now. Keeping the girls too occupied to think about it is what today was all about. But the reality that Les could still die took a back seat in my mind to all the promises I've been making to Cindy and Gina that their big sister would be home someday and be good as new."

"Matt, you know the ones who die of this aren't usually caught this early on. We talked about that. So did her counselors. I don't know how I know, but she's going to get better. Believe that. I do."

He looked into her eyes, and suddenly so did he. He believed it to the depth of his soul. Then, his mind at ease, something else invaded his thoughts. Matt sat transfixed. The moonlight in Justine's hair made it look like strands of spun gold—a shade he wouldn't have thought possible. And once again that incredible aura of peace that surrounded her seeped into his soul. She looked like an angel, though he was also very aware she was all too human.

"Thanks," he said, it seemed and it was the most natural thing in the world to lean toward her and cover her lips with his.

He didn't linger. Didn't have to. Just as she knew his child would prosper and come home whole, he knew there was something special and right happening between them. It didn't need to be rushed or analyzed. It just was.

# *Chapter Nine*

He'd kissed her, Justine thought again the next day as she filled the huge thermos she'd borrowed from the church. Hot chocolate. Cold turkey sandwiches. Hot pasta salad to round out the meal. Cupcakes to top it off. Sort of the way the kiss had topped off Harvest Fest. It was a thank-you kind of kiss, she assured herself. Hadn't he said "Thanks" just before his lips touched hers?

*But he kissed you on the lips,* a little voice inside her head reminded her.

Matt was a man. Just because the last person to kiss her on the lips thought it was a prelude to more didn't mean Matt did. That last kiss had come from a boy. And it had been a lot of years ago. She was a different person now. That part of her was locked away, and Matt was a different person altogether from that long-ago boy. He had the weighty responsibility of being a single parent to three children. Starting a relationship was the last thing he'd be interested in. He'd asked for a friend. He needed a friend. And that was all the kiss had meant.

Friendship.

Gina and Cindy shrieked as the kite Matt had launched dipped dangerously, but then a gust of wind took it up high into the cloudless sky. Laughing, Matt turned back to her and accepted the cup of hot chocolate she'd just poured for him. She ignored the little tingle the touch of his fingers sent racing up her arm. He tapped his white foam cup against hers and parroted her secret mantra of the day.

''To friendship,'' he said, confirming what she'd known in her heart all along. The children were his main focus, now and always. She was just a friend.

''To friendship,'' she said, and wished she knew why she felt so keen a disappointment blooming inside her. She wasn't interested in being more than a friend to this man and his daughters. She had a career she loved and a church family to care for. She had no time for a deeper relationship with Matt. Or the instant motherhood that came along with him.

She watched the girls follow the kite and felt rather than saw Matt roll to his feet.

"Closer," he shouted, cupping his hands around his mouth. "Let the string out and get back this way."

"Those cliffs make me nervous, too," she admitted, and he gave her a grateful smile.

"No, they don't. Reverend Burns told me you used to climb them."

"Which is how I know they can be dangerous. Do you think Cindy would be insulted if we joined them?"

"I don't think you could insult one of my kids. At the risk of sounding blasphemous, you hung the moon and just might walk on water."

"No, that's my boss. But as they have such an inflated opinion of me, let's take advantage. I've never flown a kite quite that impressive."

"I guess I got a little carried away."

Thinking of the enormous nylon kite with the five-foot wingspan that was currently swooping toward the sea like a giant bird of prey, she knew that was a true understatement. Matt might not need a wife to help raise his kids, but he had probably relied on Diane Trent to curb his male tendency to overspend.

"What's the smirk for?" Matt demanded, obviously trying to look offended and failing. She had caught on to his teasing from the first. Absently, she wondered why that was.

"I hear you promised Cindy a bike for her birthday. Do yourself and her a favor and take her with you. That way she'll reach the pedals before her thirteenth birthday.''

"Les has a big mouth. When did she tell you that?''

"While you were talking to the psychiatrist. She had a good idea they were going to recommend she stay. I got instructions not to let you get carried away, in case she wasn't there to stop you.''

"She was always such a good kid. Never any real trouble at all from the day she was born,'' he said, shaking his head as they walked toward the girls. "Diane used to say she was teaching us to be parents gently. I guess that's why this whole anorexia thing blindsided me. Cindy and Gina you expect to act out, but not Les. Never Les,'' he muttered.

He loped ahead as Cindy let go of the line and Gina lifted off from the ground. Gina screamed, and Cindy jumped up, caught the string and settled her little sister back on earth.

"That was mean, young lady—'' Matt began to scold.

"Do it again,'' Gina shouted. "Let go. Let go. I can fly.''

Tired, Justine sank to the grass and watched Matt skillfully handle his role of father and playmate. Who knew children were this exhausting in a nonchurch setting? She smiled. And she'd promised the girls she would share dinner with the family before tonight's church service. For a few fool-

ish moments she wished there was no Sunday
evening service scheduled. And that thought worried her.

Dinner at Matt's house was over, and Justine
had volunteered to finish up the dishes while Matt
ran out to pick up some milk and bread for the
morning. As she finished rinsing the last pot, she
checked her watch. Six. Still plenty of time to get
home and change for the service.

The phone rang and she hesitated to answer it.
But then, thinking Cindy had already gotten in the
tub and knowing Matt had a rule against Gina answering the phone at her tender age, Justine lifted
the receiver.

"…*accept a collect call from*— Say yes," Leslie shouted at the other end of the line.

"Y-yes," Cindy said, surprise and uncertainty
in her tone.

"Good girl, Cindy," Leslie said, before Justine
could reveal her presence on the line.

"Hi! Are you okay? Kristin Griffin took over
your part in the play. She wasn't nearly—"

"Listen, Cindy," Leslie cut in. "I don't have
time for old home week right now. I need you to
do me a big favor."

"Oh. Well, sure."

Justine could hear the hurt in the nine-year-old's
voice. She felt like a spy but knew Leslie might
still have a few tricks in her arsenal. Spying, she'd

told Matt, was okay if it saved a child's life. Realizing she'd trivialized the difficulty, she fervently prayed Matt would get back soon. She thought it might be better to get Cindy off the phone instead of finding out what Leslie was up to. Silently, anxiously, Justine hung on.

"I need help getting out of here," Leslie told Cindy.

Matt walked in, and Justine motioned him to be silent as she flipped the phone to the speaker setting.

"But Daddy says you're sick and that you're in a hospital so you can get better," Cindy argued. "Besides, how could I help you? I'm just a kid."

"I want you to tell Daddy you're mad at him for making me stay here. Maybe he'd need me to come home if you cause Miss Neal all kinds of trouble."

Matt took the receiver from Justine's unresistant fingers. "Busted, Leslie," he snapped, before she could continue with her inventive little plan. "How could you tell your sister to do something like that? Now, tell Cindy you're sorry for trying to get her in trouble, and hang up the phone."

"Sorry, Cindy," Leslie said, sounding more disgusted with getting caught than she did apologetic. "It's your fault, Dad," she accused, the second Cindy clicked off the line. "If you hadn't locked me in here, I wouldn't—"

"Stop right there," Matt cut in. "I'm very disappointed that you'd try to use your sister this way. I can't handle talking to you right now. I'm just too angry. I'm hanging up now, since you didn't," he told her, and disconnected the call. He stood there staring at the phone and shaking his head. "I don't know her at all anymore, do I? How could I lose a child practically overnight?"

The phone rang again before Justine could formulate an answer. Truthfully, she doubted there was one. It might actually be the most universally asked and unanswered question in the history of the world. She imagined her own mother had asked it.

Matt lifted the receiver, a resigned look on his face, and punched a button that accepted the collect call. "No. I'm not bringing you home…I *do* love you. Therefore, I'm not letting you leave there till you're better…I'm sorry you miss us. We miss you, too, but you need to stay there and get your head straight. Don't call here again tonight. I won't accept any more collect calls. Neither will anyone else. And these two will be coming out of your allowance once you do come home. Good night, princess. I love you."

Grimly, he put down the phone and stood just staring at it again. "I'll have to call the administrator and see that she doesn't have access to the phone. I can't let her drag Cindy into her bad behavior, and I don't want my in-laws interfering."

Justine nodded. "You haven't lost her and you

did the right thing. Just now, and when you signed her into the Mittler Center. You go see to the girls. I'll let myself out. I wish I could stay, but I have to get to the church.''

Pursing his lips, he nodded. ''Free for lunch tomorrow?''

She didn't have the heart to turn him down. ''Noon at Harry's.''

Matt stood as Justine rushed into Harry's Kitchen at lunchtime on Monday. She was fifteen minutes late, looked harried, angry and gorgeous. ''Bad morning?'' he asked.

''Tell me, why does every town have a busybody-hypocrite masquerading as a pillar of their community and church?''

''So chiefs of police and ministers everywhere can earn stars for their heavenly crowns,'' Matt explained so patiently that he cracked himself and her up.

''She made me late. I hate to be late,'' Justine said, pouting while trying not to laugh. Matt grinned. Her staid facade simply crumbled when she pouted, just as it did when she was with his children. He wondered if she knew, but decided not to mention it.

''Don't sweat being late. It gave me time to snag a booth and grill Harry on his selections of the day. Besides, I'll just take fifteen minutes extra today. On principle,'' he said emphatically. His morning hadn't been all sunshine and roses, either, thanks to Geneve Peterson. He sighed. "I know you can't say who your annoying visitor was, but I have a good idea, anyway. I'm sorry. She hit my office at nine. I'd had my coffee by then, but it didn't make being lectured by that woman any easier to take. The extra fifteen is in protest for the headache she gave me. What was she-who-shall-remain-nameless on her high horse with you about?"

"Oh, no. You start. You had to put up with her first."

Now that he'd had time to think, he could see the humor. Matt tried to look serious, but it was hard to keep a straight face.

"Ah! Where to start? Let's see—neglecting my job by refusing to investigate Nathan Taylor, the man she blames for chasing Charles out of town, and unleashing my incompetent self on the town."

He shook his head at the irony of her next complaint. Only he knew about the call he'd gotten from his old boss in the Green Bay FBI Bureau office when he'd tried to trace the corporation that bought the apartments. He'd been told everything was safe for his citizens and that the FBI's involvement with the corporation was of a protective nature. He'd backed off, knowing how testy the Bureau got when a local tread where they weren't wanted.

"She moved on to my second failing," he continued. "I have yet to discover who the true and

no doubt nefarious new owner of the Harbor
Apartments is. I also disgraced my ill-gotten uniform on Saturday by gambling at the Harvest Festival.''

Comically, Justine slapped the back of her hand
against her forehead, shaking her head. "Oh, say
it's not so!"

"*And* I allowed my children to gamble, as well."
He grinned. "I really can't see carnival games as
gambling but according to Miss Peterson, I should
have been making arrests at the festival, you see, not
supplying Cindy and Gina with the ill-gotten gains
of my gambling and…oh, corrupting them. And I
was also corrupting our young and impressionable
minister.''

"Oh, please! Reverend Burns should have done
something about that woman years ago."

"I remind you she's a woman." He looked mis-
chievous. "Your new territory."

Justine regarded him with a jaundiced eye. "I
wouldn't be surprised to find out that she's the reason I got the post with First Peninsula."

"What?" He couldn't see Geneve Peterson trying to help Justine in any way. He hadn't told her
half of what the woman had said about seeing them
together. He was just glad Miss Peterson apparently had been too much a coward to make those
charges to Justine's face. He wouldn't want to see
Justine hurt in any way.

"Don't let that kindly face fool you. Reverend

Burns can be downright sneaky,'' Justine teased. ''You have to admit, he no longer has to deal with her Monday morning tirades, uh…I mean visits,'' she hastened to correct herself, her smile broadening.

''Ah. In that case, I just may have to send her flowers if she's the reason you're still here. So what did the old busybody want with you? Or was it pretty much the same thing?''

''Except that I should use my influence with the Women's League to put an end to the festival. I should also work to stamp out sin and corruption within town government, not befriend it.'' She sputtered and covered her mouth before looking back up. ''Oh. I shouldn't laugh. But she was a bitter old woman even when he was in high school, according to Reverend Burns. I know she was when *I* was in high school. I've been trying to kill her with kindness as he suggested, but it isn't working.''

Matt chuckled. ''That's a shame because, when you came in here with steam coming out of your ears, I could see how badly you want to succeed.''

Justine stared at him. He could tell her mind was working, and knew she'd picked up his hidden meaning when she let out a quiet but unladylike snort of laugher.

''You're terrible, Matthew Trent. But thanks for helping me laugh at it all. So, what's Harry got for us today?''

\* \* \*

Late Thursday afternoon, Matt trudged up the steps on his way to Justine's office, eager to see her. He hadn't had time to talk to her since Monday. He was too early to pick up Cindy and Gina, and he needed a few minutes with Justine. He'd just gotten back to town from his first family counseling session with Leslie. It had been a disaster. At least, as far as he was concerned, even though the therapist had seemed pleased.

Justine was sitting behind her desk, frowning down at a yellow legal pad filled with her fluid script. Shaking her head, Justine scratched something out, then wrote a new word above the old. He hated to disturb her, but he'd promised to let her know how Les was doing. And selfishly, he needed her just then.

"Hi, you got a minute?" he asked, after watching her for several moments.

Justine's head snapped up. "Matt!" She paused, and he could see her studying him. "Uh-oh. How was the meeting, or shouldn't I ask?"

Matt hadn't realized he was that transparent. He walked the rest of the way into her office and sank into one of the two chairs in front of her desk. "It was my worst nightmare. I keep drawing that analogy, don't I? Do me a favor. Pinch me. Wake me up."

"I'm sorry it was hard."

"Today made that scene when we were leaving

her there feel like a picnic. I'm never going to get used to hearing how much she hates me.''

Justine tossed her pen down, her eyes sparking. ''You know, I don't think you should have to. I'd like to go see her. Sheila Kiley called me yesterday wanting my input as Leslie's pastor. She'd gotten my name from Leslie. Dr. Kiley told me she'd like me to visit as often as I can. I wanted to talk to you about it first. I'll give her a call if you'd like.''

''If you think you can get through to that kid of mine, I'm game.''

''I can but try.''

# Chapter Ten

Matt glanced up at the knock on his office door the following Monday. Justine stood in the doorway looking more like a fashion model than a minister. She had one hand braced on the door frame and in the other she held the long strap of her shoulder bag. He jumped to his feet, thrilled to see her.

"Justine, come in. Sit." He motioned toward the chair on the other side of his desk. It was filled with a pile of old files one of his deputies had dumped off for him earlier. "Oh. Sorry. Things are still a little disorganized around here, and we're running out of storage. I'm trying to move us into the twenty-first century by scanning this stuff onto CDs," he explained as he moved around the desk and scooped the files up, looking for somewhere to put them. He spied his empty trash can. It wasn't a perfect solution, but whatever worked.

Justine chuckled, and Matt gritted his teeth against the desire flooding his bloodstream. It wasn't fair for a minister to be able to do that to a man with one little laugh. She should have been made to turn it in when she was ordained or something. Anything. The least the powers that be could have done was banned her from laughing!

"Now, there's one solution to the storage crisis. Let the landfill handle it. I never thought of that," she said, inclining her head toward the now full trash can.

Matt looked down, realizing the implication of what he'd done. "Very funny, Rev. Charles wasn't much for computers. The paper explosion in here is twenty-five years' worth of reports on petty vandalism and truancies. Some of these are probably files on people who have become model citizens."

Justine arched an eyebrow. "Some of this is probably courtesy of me, and I like to think *I* am."

He grinned. "Believe me when I say that as a parent I take courage from that. So, what brings you here?"

"I'm on my way to see Leslie. I wanted you to know, and I wanted to show you the pictures the girls drew for her today. Gina's is a big flower in the rain." She grimaced. "I made the mistake of thinking it was an umbrella. But Cindy's is pretty incredible."

She handed him the drawing of the lighthouse with a cross on top. The rays of light came from the cross rather than the bulb beneath. Written with painstaking care at the bottom were these words: *"I am the light of the world. He who follows Me shall not walk in darkness, but have the light of life.* John 8:12"

"Our copy machine is on the fritz. I thought you might like a copy. I know I would. The Women's League could adopt that as a logo since they meet at the lighthouse. What I don't understand is why Cindy wasn't more interested in Kit's art if she has such a flare for it. Or was she just more interested in the rides?"

"I don't think that was it. She doesn't think she's any good. I tell her she is, but—" he shook his head "—she doesn't believe me. When we first saw Kit's mural at the church, she measured her own work against it. I told her she couldn't compare her artwork to an adult artist's work, but she wasn't buying it."

Justine frowned. "You've given me an idea. Maybe getting Les to look outside herself a little would help her right now. Do you mind if I talk to her about this?"

"Not at all. I hope I'm not seeing trouble where there isn't any, but this could be a self-esteem problem with Cindy, too. I honestly don't understand it. I praise every one of their accomplishments. I try not to be critical of them if something they do isn't perfect. And Diane was a great mother. She was positive and upbeat with them even when she knew she was dying. They were her greatest joy.''

''What about your in-laws? You said they used to spend a lot of time with the girls.''

''As annoyed as I am with them, neither of them would ever knowingly harm the kids in any way.''

''I'm not thinking it would have been knowingly. What was their relationship like with Diane?''

''One to envy. In their eyes, the sun rose and set on Di. And that's a direct quote from her father. Why?''

''I had a friend in divinity school who had zero confidence in herself. I'd met her parents. Like you with your girls, they were wonderful with her. Praised her. Were obviously proud of her. But she had this older sister who had died in an auto accident her last year of college. Let me tell you, after a week at their house one summer, I understood. No one could have lived up to that icon of a sister.''

''You think my in-laws loved Diane and praised her memory so much that Les and Cindy think they suffer by comparison?'' He slapped the desk. ''I used Diane as my measure of a woman when I was talking to Les about dieting. She and her mother were so close. I thought if she saw Diane's weight as acceptable, she'd knock off the dieting.'' He could feel the blood drain from his head and his stomach flipped sickly. "Idiot! Di weighed, like, ninety pounds by the time she died. I didn't want to remember her that way. I guess I succeeded, but maybe Les didn't. Did I do this to her?"

Justine shook her head and reached across the desk, laying her hand over his, which was fisted on the desk. "There you go again. Don't do this to yourself. Leslie had this problem before you talked to her about dieting, and your in-laws loved their daughter and wanted her children to remember how wonderful she was. There's no blame here. Only healing." She checked her watch. "And now I'm off to Green Bay to see if I can't facilitate a little of that healing."

"Tell me, what is your connection to Leslie?" Sheila Kiley asked as she regarded Justine with a shrewd gaze.

Justine blinked. They'd spoken on the phone. Kiley had encouraged her to visit Leslie. "I thought you knew. It was you who called me."

"At the time I thought I knew. I didn't connect the youth pastor, Reverend Clemens, with Justine, the woman who accompanied Leslie and her father the day she was admitted. I'm just trying to understand fully what Mr. Trent means when he says you're a friend. I have to ask if there's likely to be fallout from your relationship with Leslie's father?"

*Relationship? Fallout?* She hadn't thought her interest in Leslie's well-being would be misinterpreted. She sat up a little straighter. Couldn't a man have a female friend? Just because she was a woman didn't mean she and Matt were—

"As I said when you called, I'm the youth pastor of their church. Leslie's pastor. Matt and I have become friends. Friends," she emphasized. "His child is troubled. I promised to look in on her. I hoped you would tell me what would be safe for me to discuss with her and what I shouldn't say, considering her problem."

Dr. Kiley nodded. "I didn't mean to be in any way insulting. But what some men mean by friend can be loosely interpreted. If you were romantically involved with Matthew Trent, Leslie could resent it, and in that case your involvement in this would backfire."

Mollified somewhat, Justine nodded but had to wonder why Dr. Kiley had gotten the idea that her relationship with Matt was beyond friendship. It was something she'd have to think about. But not right now. Right now, Leslie was more important.

They talked for the better part of an hour, and Dr. Kiley finally gave Justine the go-ahead to talk with Leslie. She explained what discussions to stay away from and how Justine could help Leslie form healthy outlooks.

Now, standing outside Leslie's door, Justine took a deep breath, said a quick prayer for guidance and knocked. In seconds a frail blonde of indeterminate age came to the door.

"I came to see Leslie," Justine told the girl.

"Sure. Leslie. Visitor," she called over her shoulder. "I'm Carrie. I'll make myself scarce. I have a meeting in a few minutes, anyway." The girl motioned Justine into the room.

Quietly, in a low voice as they passed each other, Carrie said, "The kid's still sulking. All of us who don't have a choice about coming here do it for a while. So don't worry. She'll come around."

"Thanks, Carrie," Justine said as she walked by the thin girl who was little more than skin stretched over bird-thin bones.

"Leslie?" Justine called, entering the suite.

Leslie walked out of her room and into the central sitting room that separated two bedrooms. The three rooms made up the lovely suite. "Reverend Clemens? How come you're here?" There was real fear in Leslie's voice and in her eyes. "Is something wrong with my sisters?" She sucked in a frightened breath. "Or my dad? He didn't get shot or anything, did he?"

"Would you care?" Justine asked, deciding that, though it was an abrupt beginning, she shouldn't let so perfect an opening pass by.

Leslie looked appropriately horrified. "Of course I care. He's my dad!"

"But you hate him. You tell him so at every opportunity."

Leslie looked away and flopped on the sofa, a scowl firmly in place. "That doesn't mean I want him dead."

Justine sat in the chair next to her. "I'm glad to hear that. I wish he knew that. It's sad that you hate him. He loves you so much."

"Right. That's why I'm here and he and my sisters are over an hour away."

"You're here because he does love you. It isn't as if your eating habits were causing a disruption in the household. In fact, you weren't costing much at all in groceries. How much do you think this place costs him each day? Try twenty percent of a thousand dollars. And tell me, how does your dad bringing you where you can get help translate to not caring about you?"

Leslie didn't answer. She just continued to sit with her arms crossed, staring at the floor, a mutinous look on her face.

"Leslie, I know this isn't easy. I know you're scared. But lashing out at your father the way you are is just plain cruel."

Leslie's head snapped up.

"Yes. Cruel. Let me ask you a question. Have you ever seen your father cry, except when your mother died?"

"He didn't cry then. Not in front of people, anyway. I heard him that night, but he didn't cry at the funeral or anything. I heard her make him promise not to.''

Oh, this was perfect. ''And you say he doesn't love you? After leaving, your father sat in his car and cried for at least five minutes. Every time you tell him you hate him it's like you've put a knife in his heart. He left here last Thursday after your family counseling session and came straight to my office. He's crushed that his little girl hates him. It's all he thinks about.''

Leslie was beginning to look a bit crushed herself, but Justine continued. ''I know your dad looks like a tough guy, but he isn't tough when it comes to his children. You've frightened him and made him doubt himself as a father. That, you didn't do on purpose. But now you've wounded him with words of hatred, and that just isn't acceptable. He's perfectly willing to bear the hurt and keep coming back for more, but it's wrong of you to do this to him. You have a wonderful father.''

Leslie sat a little straighter and defiance sparked in her eyes. She crossed her arms and smirked. ''You sound a little jealous, Reverend.''

Perhaps Sheila Kiley hadn't been too far off the mark. A relationship between them was clearly not a good idea for Leslie, even if it were for the two of them. Which it wasn't, she hasten to remind herself. Justine responded the only way she could. She kept it on Leslie's level and let the true charge go right over her head as if it hadn't registered.

''Maybe I am. When I was Gina's age, my father walked out on my mother and me. He just disappeared. I never saw him again. I would have given anything, when I was growing up, for a father like you have, and yet you seem determined to toss him away. I can't understand that.''

Leslie deflated like a popped balloon. ''Daddy cried? You're sure?''

''I was with him. I once heard a quote that I think was very wise. A parent is only as happy as their saddest child. You've been pretty sad. Haven't you?''

Tears filled the girl's jade-green eyes. ''Everything fell apart,'' she sobbed. ''We were so happy. Then Mommy got sick. For a while they told us it would all be okay, then they told us she was only going to get sicker till God took her to be with Him. Cindy and I didn't want her to go, but by the time she did, we knew she'd be happier. It was just that we wouldn't be. Nanna and Grandpa came over all the time and it was nice to see them, until Dad started getting mad about it.''

''Do you understand why he was annoyed with them?''

Leslie shrugged. ''Not really. It was weird. After a while, he'd show up...you know...come home from work. And if they were there, he'd get all tense. His smile would sort of change and he'd be all stiff and formal. He was never like that before Mommy died or even right after.''

"Did they ever step on his toes?"

"Huh?"

"Oh, come on, you know. Things like, he'd say you couldn't have a CD player and they'd buy you one, anyway."

Leslie fiddled with the bottom button of her top. "I guess. Clothes and toys and stuff. But it wasn't just that. He'd say things about them coming by and sending the baby-sitter home. They'd try to laugh at his grumpy mood, but it was like they couldn't please him anymore."

"Has your dad ever done you a favor you didn't want?"

She pulled a face. "Yeah. He stuffed me in this place, didn't he?"

Not wanting to let the conversation go off track but just as determined not to let an opportunity slip by, Justine nodded. "At least you see it as a favor now."

"No, I do not!" Leslie snapped, insulted that Reverend Clemens could think she was dumb enough to fall for a trick like that.

Reverend Clemens didn't get angry that she'd raised her voice the way her dad or even her Nanna would. She just shrugged.

"Okay, that'll serve as my point, then. Your father didn't ask your grandparents to show up almost every day when he was trying to work out a new life for all of you. They'd raised their daughter. Now it was your father's privilege to raise you three. And he was going to have to do that in a way he hadn't expected and certainly hadn't asked for with your mom gone. Unfortunately, he couldn't get on with that job because they were interfering.''

Hearing it from her father's side, Leslie got a funny feeling in her stomach. It felt like being hungry, so she pushed it away. ''Now we can't see them at all,'' she protested. ''Not since they asked us to come live with them.''

Reverend Clemens nodded as if she agreed, but then said, ''Suppose I told you your next-door neighbors have asked Gina to move in with them?''

Shocked to her toes, Leslie cried, ''She's my sister!''

''Relax. It didn't happen. But see how it felt? All three of you are your father's children. He had a right to be angry. You don't ask a child a question like that when you haven't cleared it with the parents first. He must have felt they were trying to take you away. Can you blame him?''

Leslie didn't like being suckered like that, even if the reverend did make her point. ''They're still our grandparents. Mommy's parents. We miss them. We saw them every day then never! And *I* don't have a say in it. *I* don't have a say in anything. I couldn't stop Mommy from dying. I couldn't stop Cindy from getting kidnapped. I couldn't stop us from having to move.''

"But life is often like that, Leslie. The best thing you can do is to put your trust in God and let Him control your life.''

Leslie rolled her eyes. "Yeah. Right. The way *Dad* does?''

"Maybe he hasn't been very good at that, but that doesn't mean God wasn't in control, anyway.''

Now, there was something she'd never understand! "God let Mommy die. He let Cindy get snatched at school. He let Dad move us to Safe Harbor and keep us from seeing Nanna and Grandpa.''

Reverend Clemens just nodded. "And He let you stop eating. I know you felt in control of that, but, if you don't mind my saying, that didn't turn out to be too good an idea. It blew up in your face and you nearly died.''

Okay. She had her there.

Then Reverend Clemens did something that brought back that funny feeling in her stomach. She smiled kind of softly and smoothed Leslie's hair off her forehead. Mommy used to do the same thing.

"Everyone has free will,'' Reverend Clemens continued, as if the world hadn't just shifted. "God, though, can use questionable decisions or bad things that happen by accident and make something good come out of them. Let's look at some of the things that have happened to your family from God's point of view.

"We'll start with your mother's death. Most people think about death in terms of how it affects them. But what about the person herself? God knows how wonderful heaven is and how happy we are once we get there."

She'd heard the expression from her dad, and Nanna said it, too. Now Leslie really knew what a lightbulb going on in your brain felt like! "So, like, dying isn't as big a deal for God?"

Reverend Clemens nodded. "Because He knows what's on the other side. But on an earthly level, He was working in your mother's life all the time. Your Dad told me that you and your sisters were your mother's greatest joy. He knew your mother only had so many days on earth, so He sent your father into her life when she was still very young. And they had you three when a lot of women don't even have one child yet."

"So you think He made sure she was happy while she was here?"

Justine grinned. She just loved it when she was able to guide a child through all the confusion to find the right spiritual conclusion.

"That's what I believe," she told Leslie. "And there are more ways He was in control. Why do you think we're here in the first place?"

"On earth?" Leslie's smooth forehead wrinkled,

deep in thought. "Well, I guess we're here to find our way to heaven. Otherwise, we wasted our time. Right?"

Justine nodded. "That's the most important one. From what I hear, your mother must have done that. Anything else?"

"To live as best as we can and honor God with the way we live our lives. Mommy did that, too."

"I only have to look at how wonderful her children are to see that she did. Anything else?" Justine urged.

"To help other people know Him."

"She certainly did that with you and your sisters. I'd say she has three souls to her credit."

Leslie giggled. The sound was as beautiful as it was confusing. What was so funny?

"And Daddy," the girl added. "He always says he was a godless heathen till he met Mommy."

*Thank you, Diane Trent, for continuing to be a shining example for your daughter and for your influence on Matt.* "Well, there you go. Is that about it?"

"We're supposed to help those less fortunate. Mom always told me that. She used to cook meals for the homeless."

"Well, I can't think of anything a Christian should do that your mother didn't get done while she was here. Can you?"

"I guess not."

"So, since this is about her and not those she

left behind, we should be happy she was able to accomplish all her goals and that now she's happy in heaven.''

''But— But why'd she have to suffer that way?''

''Maybe so she'd be able to leave you and your sisters behind with no regrets. She was ready to move on to a better place by then. You said her death was easier for all of you for the same reason. Maybe that was why. Or maybe, through all her suffering, she learned something deep in her heart that she never shared with anyone. Maybe that was the one thing she had left to learn before she went to heaven.''

Justine went on to point out that God would eventually use their move to Safe Harbor for good, even though it hadn't made Leslie happy yet. Which would in turn mean Cindy's abduction had happened for good reason.

Though Justine already thought God had used the move for good, she knew Leslie wasn't ready to hear how fortunate it was that her anorexic tendencies had been discovered. She did promise to talk to Matt, when the opportunity presented itself, about the girls seeing their grandparents. It was a promise she wasn't looking forward to keeping, considering how betrayed Matt felt by the Gainers.

# *Chapter Eleven*

In the anonymity of the darkened theater Matt was free to look his fill of Justine. She sat next to him, engrossed in the byplay on the big screen. Her attention was every bit as rapt as Cindy and Gina's. Who would guess her serene, conservative, ministerial public image hid a lively, funny, animated-film junky?

He nearly laughed out loud, remembering her defense of the hot fudge sundae lunch he'd caught her digging into with juvenile gusto when he'd walked into her office one day last week. With a perfectly straight face she'd asked what else a minister should be partial to but "sundaes." He grinned again now, adding hot-fudge-sundae addict and chocoholic to his list of her surprising traits.

"Ice cream next door afterward?" he asked.

She beamed him a hopeful smile. "You think Gina will stay awake long enough this time?"

Matt leaned forward and checked on his youngest daughter, who was sitting on Justine's left. Gina's eyes were as big as saucers following the adventure on the screen. He would not be carrying her out like last Saturday. "Oh, yeah. This is right up her alley. Horses. Indians. A cavalry chase. She's not falling asleep this time."

"Last week's film was too tame, I suppose," Justine whispered.

"Cindy got to pick last week. She's the animal lover."

"Ah. Well, to tell you the truth, nothing does me in the way talking animals do. That was a great flick, too," she finished absently as the screen captured her attention again. "Ooh. That rat! Give it to him, Spirit!" Justine urged the hero-horse of the movie.

Matt just missed stifling a snort, and got hit in the nose with a piece of Justine's popcorn in retaliation. He caught it deftly and munched it, liking his punishment just fine when she blessed him with another huge smile.

Now that he'd given up trying to do God's work by controlling every aspect of his life and the lives of his children, Matt saw how foolish it had been to panic about pursuing a relationship with Justine. She would never harm his kids. Nor would he stand in the way of her work or do anything to hurt her or her reputation. Which was why he'd decided to court her with Cindy and Gina along as chaperones. And it was easier this way since he was so incredibly out of practice at dating. In fact, he'd yet to actually ask her out. He always just suggested a fun activity and used the kids and Leslie's absence as an excuse.

He was glad of the time they'd spent together, though, because he could see how perfectly she fit into his family. The odd thing was, she completed him as Di never had. Though Justine was wonderful with his little girls and had helped Leslie tremendously even with that first visit, his feelings for Justine had more to do with how she made him feel as a man. Sure, she'd be as excellent a mother and as wonderful a second half of a parent partnership as Di had been or he'd never have moved their relationship forward. But Justine's main appeal was personal.

Friendship and tenderness had been the earmark of his relationship with Di. He felt those things for Justine, too, but she kept his emotions bouncing all over the place in a way that was unsettling but irresistibly exciting and intriguing. When he was upset, she was a balm to his spirit, but most of the time her nearness kept his heart pounding deeply. And then, just when he'd get used to that heightened sense of awareness, they'd accidently touch or she'd let out one of those sensual chuckles of hers and his heart would go skittering off a mile a minute. He'd never felt so alive.

His life had pretty much evened out in the past couple of weeks, after the turmoil of Leslie's diagnosis. Leslie had called him on her therapist's phone right after Justine's first visit to the clinic. Contrite, Leslie had tearfully apologized for making him a target of her anger, confusion and fear. Since then, his oldest daughter had improved by leaps and bounds, thrilling her counselors and doctors.

Alan had even settled down and had turned out to be a pretty decent kid, though his parents hadn't improved at all. Alan showing up at church last Sunday for services with his sister had caused more than one adult head to turn. There was more than a little hope for both kids in spite of their questionable home life.

Matt had only one baffling problem these days. While their pint-size chaperones safeguarded Justine's reputation and kept him from jumping into a serious relationship too quickly, Matt worried that she would think he saw her only as a replacement for Di. And nothing could be further from the truth. He wanted her in his life for only one reason: he could no longer imagine not having her there.

Lunch a couple of times a week for the past two weeks, when his kids were occupied in school, were the only times they'd been alone—if eating a quick meal in a booth at Harry's Kitchen could be considered being alone. This was hardly the courtship a woman dreamed of. It wasn't one Matt had ever dreamed of conducting, either, but he just couldn't seem to make the leap to formally ask her on a real, full-fledged date!

Since lunches were all they could have right now, he was determined to at least make the next one a real date at The Bistro. Maybe he'd ask her soon.

But tonight, when the movie ended, they'd all troop next door for hot fudge sundaes and a critique of the movie that, thanks to the girls, would undoubtedly be accompanied by lots of laughter.

Though Matt tried to get away for a long lunch on Monday, it was not to be. The station house was shorthanded because a flu bug had blown into town with the approaching winter, so he had to fill in. He ate lunch while on the phone with Dr. Sheila Kiley. It wasn't until five-fifteen that Matt poked his head into Justine's office—a man on a mission.

She was behind her desk, staring out her darkened window as she chewed on the cap of her pen. Her hair shimmered in the lamp light, and her mind seemed as far away.

"Hey, Rev. How was your day?" he asked.

Justine swiveled toward him, a smile automatically curving her full lips. "I just talked to Leslie. Honestly, Matt, she sounds wonderful."

"Was it another long chat about nothing or a continuation of your most recent deep, theological debate?"

Her smile broadened and she leaned her elbows on the desk, lacing her fingers under her chin. "Actually, it was girl talk, a progress report, an invitation and a request for a favor all rolled into one."

Matt took the chair across from her. "Oh?"

"She says they think she's ready to go to that private school they have a relationship with."

Matt nodded. "Yeah. Dr. Kiley called me about it this afternoon. That became my lunch break. She also said Les is gaining weight nicely. All of them are really positive about her progress and her chances. So now we've covered the progress report part, and I know the girl talk was probably way out of my league. But what was the invitation Les extended and what kind of favor is she trying to get you to do? She did ask a favor, right? Or am I not supposed to ask?"

"Even though they don't discuss the weight she's gaining with her, Leslie can tell her clothes are getting tight. I'm afraid the favor actually has to do with you. Or, more precisely, with permission to do damage to your credit card. Les wants me to take her for new clothes, and it needs to be soon since she's starting school."

Matt had to smile. That sounded so normal and wonderful. And Leslie seemed to think as much of

Justine as his other two kids did. Doubly wonderful! Without a word he reached into his pocket and pulled his credit card out of his wallet. He flipped it onto her desk blotter and named a figure—their shopping allowance.

"Wow, will you adopt me?"

"I'll take you to dinner but that's as far as I'll go," he quipped, just managing to resist countering with a proposal that would have her joining his family but in another capacity altogether.

Justine checked her watch. "It's that late already? Where was my mind? The girls are probably all packed up and ready to go." She stood. "Got any guesses what Harry's serving tonight?"

Matt took that as a yes on dinner. "I…uh…I asked Miss Neal to come over after I get them their dinner. I thought maybe we'd hit The Bistro. Call it a thank-you for taking Les shopping."

"Matt, this is kind of you but isn't necessary. Shopping with Leslie will be fun."

"So speaks someone who has yet to go shopping with my daughter. Believe me. I'll owe you weeks of meals after this. Besides, my two youngest are thrilled to be rid of me for a night. I'm afraid I've been overcompensating for Les being gone. Last night Cindy told me she's sick of my face."

Justine laughed. "She did complain to me about a certain father monopolizing all her time."

Matt grinned and looked at his watch. "So, can you be ready by seven?"

"Seven."

Matt didn't think she looked at all sure. And why would she? How could she know how to react if the meal made no sense? Jon-Paul had worked overtime to make evenings at his restaurant romantic and intimate. You might take your daughter's pastor to dinner to thank her for her help, but not to a place like The Bistro. Matt mentally kicked himself all the way to his car, while giving half an ear to the girls as they chattered on about their day.

What was the matter with him? Why had he made a stupid excuse like paying her back for shopping? Why hadn't he just said he wanted to take her out for a meal? That he loved her. That he wanted her for his wife. Half the town was making book on who'd get married first. Nathan and Constance, or him and Justine. And he'd yet to ask her out on an official date! True, the townfolk were rushing things…but he was dragging his feet.

Somehow he had to find the courage to tell her how he felt about her.

Justine checked her hair, then let her gaze shift downward to her dress again. It was pale blue silk with a skirt that flared from a princess line bodice. It had a scoop neckline trimmed in a braided rope of tiny pearls, and the long sleeves ended with the same trim at tapered cuffs.

It was modest enough by most people's standards, but Justine was always most nervous about her mode of dress when it came to the impression she made. She knew it was perfect for a fancy dinner, but that didn't stop the second, third and fourth thoughts about its appropriateness from haunting her.

When she'd gone shopping with Constance, the older woman had dismissed Justine's worry with a careless wave of her hand, saying Justine was a woman first and that the dress was feminine, not sexy. Shopping with Constance had been fun and oddly bonding, and she counted the woman as a friend. Justine smiled, remembering that moment when Constance had taken charge of her dithering companion and marched to the salesgirl with the dress. ''She'll take it and that purse you showed us to go with it,'' she'd ordered, while Justine was still dressing and unable to protest.

Now, looking at her reflection, she swirled the flared skirt about her calves and admitted the truth. Loving the dress, she hadn't really want to protest at all.

Thinking of fun shopping trips brought Leslie to mind, and worry creased her brow. After what Dr. Kiley had said that first day, maybe she should have turned down this date with Matt. And it *was* a date, no matter what he'd used as an excuse.

Justine could no longer pretend the invitations to movies, ice cream, lunch and all the other outings they'd shared had been anything but dates. Most of their time together had been shared with two adorable chaperones, but now, Justine was fairly sure Matt must have meant each and every outing as more.

Caught deep in thought, Justine jumped sky-high, catapulted from her reverie by the too-loud lobby buzzer resounding through her apartment. She looked out her window and, seeing the car parked in the lot, buzzed Matt in. She stopped at the mirror to check her hair again and groaned, tossing the comb back on the hall table. What was wrong with her?

Matthew Trent.

The answer echoed from deep in her heart. And she accepted the truth. She cared far too much about what he thought of her. What he *felt* for her. These were emotions she hadn't tasted since her difficult adolescent years during the first rush of womanhood. Even then, without the guiding force of the Lord in her heart, she'd shied from this, fearing she would follow her mother's path to personal destruction.

Since then, everything in her life had changed— except that. She closed her eyes. She was still so afraid. *Guide me, Lord. Strengthen me. What do I do about Matt?*

Unfortunately, no answer came, which she knew

could be her answer. So with no antidote for her feelings of nervous anticipation and worry, Justine went to her door when the bell rang.

"Hi," she said as she swung the door open. Once she caught sight of him, Justine was thankful she'd greeted Matt before she really saw him.

Because the sight left her speechless.

He wore a dark gray suit, snowy white shirt and silvery gray tie. Theirs was a fairly casual church, so she'd never seen him in anything more formal than a sport coat or his uniform. That had been appealing enough. Jeans had been the best. Or so she'd thought till now!

*Lord, You worked overtime when You picked out his particular genes. But didn't You forget something? Like a label for the unsuspecting? "Dangerous to the faint of heart—could be addictive."*

Justine's mind was clear enough to notice a moment of awkward silence as Matt just stared back at her. She couldn't seem to rally her faculties enough to break it. Her mind was racing. Was the dress wrong, after all? Too fancy? Too something?

"You… Wow," Matt said at last.

Justine fumbled with her neckline. "It's okay? I wasn't sure, but Constance said—"

Matt grinned in a way that put Justine's thoughts at ease about her dress but her senses more on edge.

"Remind me to thank her for her influence. You ready?"

She remembered her mother telling her to always keep a man waiting, but Justine was ready and had long ago dismissed any advice her mother had given about men. "Just let me grab my purse and cape," she told Matt, and rushed to her room.

"There may be a storm moving in," he called after her, "or not. The weather bureau wasn't really clear about what to expect tonight."

Justine chuckled. "When are they ever sure?" she said over her shoulder and her nerves eased a bit more. Why had she been so apprehensive? Matt was the easiest person to talk to. They never ran out of interesting conversations and had yet to find a topic on which they didn't ultimately agree.

When she returned from the bedroom with her cape and purse, Justine found Matt looking out the front window down at the well-lit parking lot below. "The new owner sure has made a lot of changes to the complex," he said as he turned back to her.

"Progress, I guess. But I won't miss the roofers when they go. *Pound. Pound. Pound.* Eight o'clock. Every morning for the past two weeks right over my head. I don't need an alarm on weekdays anymore. You could set a clock by those guys."

"Have you been told what comes next?" he asked as he opened the door to the hall.

"The letter we all got in September promised the halls would be papered and painted, and new carpets installed. But that's on the inside. Nothing has changed the general look of the place as much as painting the trim and shutters a new color and putting those adorable miniature rocky bluffs and lighthouses in front of all the entrances. It looks to me as if the new owners, mysterious though they still are, are living up to promises.''

"What do you think of the change in name? I hear a few die-hard residents were annoyed.''

She shrugged. "Consider the source of that dissent. Our post office addresses stayed the same, so I don't see the problem. And I kind of like Harbor Quay,'' she said as they stopped at his car. "It plays up the whole maritime theme.''

Matt looked across the lot at the new, more nautical-style sign guarding the entrance. "Yeah, Harbor Quay has pizzazz.''

Justine shot him a wry grin. "Now you sound like your eldest.''

Matt chuckled and opened the passenger door of the unmarked navy police cruiser he drove most places. "Guilty. *Pizzazz* was her word, not mine. But I agree with her.''

"So do I,'' Justine said as he shut her door. "I think the real problem people have is the owners and their secretive nature,'' she continued when Matt climbed behind the wheel.

He shrank the interior space all out of proportion to his wide shoulders. She'd come to the conclusion the first time she'd sat next to him in the car that the shrinking-space phenomenon had more to do with the force of his charisma than his size.

"I have to admit, any kind of secrecy bothers me," Matt confided. "These mystery owners sure do."

"And I hate to admit how ridiculous *this* is, but Geneve Peterson has me thinking overtime—especially when I'm trying to fall asleep. Her wild imagination put mine into overdrive. I actually had a nightmare last week about a drug smuggling terrorist wearing an apron, standing at my door demanding to borrow a cup of sugar at gunpoint."

Matt burst out laughing.

Justine blushed and was glad for the darkened car. "I said it was ridiculous!"

"Believe me," Matt said, still trying to control his laughter, "you can relax. I finally broke down and tried to trace the corporation. I'm told they're legit. But if you have any more of those dreams, let me know. I can always use a good laugh."

She folded her arms, trying to look annoyed, but his laughter was contagious and her helpless smile took the edge off her act. "I'll be sure to let you know. Actually, I'd like to thank whoever it is. At least it focused some of the gossip and speculation away from Nathan and Constance. Honestly, she had a right to stop dating Chief Creasy."

"Creasy seemed like a nice enough guy," Matt commented of his predecessor.

"But so is Nathan."

"I agree, from the little I've seen. I just hope there's nothing funny about him. I never gave it a thought until—"

At Matt's abrupt halt, Justine finished with the only possible ending to that sentence. "Geneve Peterson complained about him, didn't she?"

Matt grinned wryly and nodded. "And she got me to thinking that where there's smoke there's often fire. A lot of people have asked where he came from. Where he goes when he leaves."

"Constance seems happy with him around. I've gotten to know her pretty well since coming back to Safe Harbor, and I think I know a happy woman when I see one. And she's no dummy. If she hasn't got a problem with the man, I don't and neither should you."

"Yes, ma'am," he said, his grin at once sheepish and teasing as he pulled into the parking lot at the edge of the bluff overlooking Lake Michigan. "Hey. There's Alex Wilkins and Holly going in the lower entrance."

Justine saw a chance to get back some of her own and tease Matt. "I know a little girl named Gina who's quite taken with Holly's twins. There's a love triangle developing in their Sunday school classroom."

"Oh, no. Don't even think of going there. I am not supposed to have to worry about boys for three more years with Les. Seven more for Cindy and *eleven* for Gina."

She shot him a dubious look.

He grinned. "I know it's wishful thinking, but you could leave a guy some glimmer of hope."

They were still bantering about parenthood and all the myths Justine had blown apart for Matt when they entered The Bistro.

Felicity Smith, acting as hostess, showed them to their reserved table. It was in Justine's favorite part of the restaurant, the second-floor dining room that had the best view of the lake. They were tucked in a little corner near the cozily lit fireplace when the young single mother gave them their menus with a friendly smile. "Have a nice meal," she said, and lit the lantern on their table. The flame danced and flickered on the warm wood-paneled walls and against the pen-and-ink sketch of a lighthouse that hung on the wall over the table.

Justine fought panic as Matt pulled out her chair to seat her and sat in the chair nearest hers rather than one of the other two chairs at the table. Their's had to be the most secluded table in the restaurant.

The place.

The table.

The reservations.

It all screamed romance. What had gotten into her? She shouldn't be there with him. She had no interest in a romance, did she?

For years the very idea of having a man in her life had been the stuff of her worst nightmares. But now, Justine couldn't deny how happy she was when she was with Matt. What was happening between them certainly didn't go with her vision for her life. And what was more confusing, their developing relationship felt more like a dream than the nightmare it should.

Once again Reverend Burns's words of wisdom the day she'd been appointed Women and Youth Pastor echoed in her mind. *"Seek His plan for your life, dear, not your own,"* he'd said. She knew she had to trust God the way she'd advised Matt to do but she was finding it was easier in theory than in execution. Matthew Trent had the power to change her life forever—and also break her heart.

# *Chapter Twelve*

"I haven't been here since Chief Creasy brought me when I was interviewing for the job," Matt said after he'd settled across from her. "The atmosphere sure improves with the company." He reached across the table to take her hand. She watched it disappear between both of his and could have sworn she felt a tremble. Trouble was, she wasn't sure if it was his hand or hers doing the shaking.

"Matt."

"Listen," he said, and cleared his throat.

His eyes held hers, and in his gaze she saw a serious discussion coming. A discussion she was afraid she wasn't ready for.

"Good evening, sir. Madam. This evening's specials…" the waiter intoned, listing several wonderful-sounding entrées.

Justine could see Matt was frustrated by the interruption, but Justine welcomed it. For just a few minutes she wanted to catch her breath and put off dealing with whatever he'd been about to say.

"What do you recommend?" Justine asked before Matt could send him away.

"The venison medallions in burgundy wine sauce are Jon-Paul's newest addition to the menu. Everyone raves about them. Also his chicken breast with capers in a white wine and lemon cream sauce are popular."

They both ordered the venison, and as the waiter left, the band Jon-Paul was trying out began playing a romantic ballad. Matt stood and held out his hand. Well, he could hardly get into a serious discussion on a dance floor, could he? Justine got to her feet and took his hand—

And realized her mistake the second they touched.

Matt enfolded her in his arms, and Justine fought to keep her breathing steady. He moved around the floor with an easy-to-follow rhythm that made dancing with him as natural as walking. Unfortunately, that left them free to talk.

"I wanted to explain about tonight," he said. "I haven't exactly been completely truthful. About us, I mean."

Justine stiffened, and her gaze flew to his face as she missed a step. "Us?"

"Yeah. As in you and me. Together here. Dancing. When we first met, I said I just wanted a friend because you seemed reluctant to get to know me as more. It wasn't exactly a lie. I did want you for a friend—but then, I was also friends with Di.''

''I think it's a good idea for husbands and wives to be friends,'' she said, then wondered if there had been a quiver in her voice.

He grinned. ''Right, and I wanted us to be *that* kind of friends. But I don't see how we can be. Di and I were friends, partners and parents. I loved her—don't get me wrong. But what I've come to realize in these past couple months is that I don't think I was *in* love with her. We were—I guess you'd call it—'loving friends.' If she had lived, I'd have been happy for the rest of my life with her. But now I see that a good relationship can be a lot more.''

Justine felt light-headed.

''With the kids,'' Matt went on, nearly mesmerizing her with his ebony eyes and husky voice, ''I don't have a lot of free time, so, uh…the movies. The lunches. Tonight. I guess what I'm trying to find out is whether you know that this is a date. That the others were, too. Right from that first lunch at Harry's.''

She'd come to the same realization earlier, so it wasn't exactly a shock. But knowing wasn't the same as hearing it from Matt himself. But, hey, dating was okay. She could do dating. It was a step. Not a leap.

"Dating's okay," she said. Her voice, however, didn't sound quite right—the quaver was more pronounced.

Matt's left eyebrow shot up. "Then, how come you sound scared to death?"

Chagrined that she should be so transparent, she admitted, "Because I am."

They had danced near the lake side of the dance floor, and suddenly, caught up in her roiling thoughts and emotions, she stepped on his foot. "Oh! I'm so sorry."

Matt chuckled, the rumbling sound in his chest close to her ear sending a delicious sort of shiver up her spine.

"Look at the beacon from the lighthouse," she said, hoping to distract him. Distract herself.

Matt's grin was all too knowing but, ever the gentleman, he didn't mention her transparent attempt at changing the subject. "Hmm. I've never seen the lighthouse from here at night. Pretty. Let's go out on the deck for a better look." He turned toward the door and put his arm around her waist, steering her that way. "We can talk out there and my spit-and-polish may survive the evening."

She followed, feeling as nervous as the first time she gave a sermon and wondering why she didn't mind.

"Wait till you see the lighthouse reflecting off the water," Justine said as they emerged onto the wooden deck.

She shivered, and Matt prayed it was the chill in the air and not fear. In spite of the Plexiglas windbreaks and the big propane heaters, it was pretty chilly out there. He took off his coat and draped it over her shoulders to warm her as they stepped to the rail. Keeping his hands on her shoulders, he stood behind her, taking in and cataloging every aspect of the night for the memory pages of his mind. He didn't want to forget a single moment.

Neither the feel of her so close to him nor the fine-boned shape of her shoulders. Neither her scent nor the texture of her silky hair as the wind floated it against his cheek.

The lake was choppy, but the light cut and danced across the water like a tangible presence. Then a gust of wind blew a cloud of vapor between them and the light. Its powerful ray split into separate beams, reminding him of Cindy's picture. "It really does seem to beacon the troubled to Safe Harbor, doesn't it? I know I was running when I came here."

"From or to?" she asked quietly.

"Hmm. I'm not sure. *From* the worry for the kids and my in-laws' intrusion. *To* what I felt was safety and a comfortable life."

"I was running, too," she admitted, her voice low. "Reverend Burns couldn't have picked a better time to need surgery. I'd just been passed over for promotion in the church where I'd served for ten years. I gave all I had to give—and they hired a man with only half my experience as a minister and none in the poor inner city. He didn't have a clue what it meant to be poor or neglected.''

*And you had all that and more to recommend you.* Matt didn't have to say it. They both knew that kind of experience couldn't be taught but had to be lived. ''I'm sorry. I didn't know there was still that kind of prejudice in the church.''

''Oh, yes. It's there. Even here. Do you really think if I'd been a man, I would have been named pastor of women and children? No.'' She shook her head. ''I'd have been straight out called assistant pastor.''

Matt didn't say anything, trying to order his thoughts. He wanted to ease her heart and buoy up her flagging spirits. ''I admit to thinking you wouldn't have been given the job of working with women and children if you hadn't been a woman. But I never considered what you might have been if you'd been a man, nor did I see your position as less than the honor it is. Your job calls for unique talents. Mothers raise the next generation with help from fathers, but we rarely do the bulk of the work the way women do. They have incredible responsibilities. I know firsthand, but I'm still an exception in this world.

''It falls to you as their pastor to listen to their

problems and help them through your influence on
their children as well as with programs like After-
School Days and your sermons. You have a special
way with children, and you're a woman so you
understand women and their problems better than
a man could. You'd almost have to. Quite frankly,
I think you have the most important job in the
church." He teased her with his grin. "Men just
tell you your role isn't vital so they, with their
fragile egos, feel more important."

Justine giggled as he had meant her to. He let
his hand drift down her arms, then back up. The
cold floated around him but didn't seem to touch
him. "Children are our most precious asset and
responsibility. Every little thing we do as parents
or secondary adults in their lives affects them."

He turned Justine in his arms. "What does it
matter what men call your contributions as long as
you're doing God's work?" He cupped her lovely
face in his palms. "I love that about you." Matt
stared into her big brown eyes…and fell.

The rest of the way under her spell.

The rest of the way in love.

He did what he'd been dying to do since the
night of Harvest Fest. He kissed her. But this time
he *did* linger. He *did* need to.

Knowing something special was growing between them was no longer enough. He needed to
know she felt the same things he did. When he

pulled her close, her arms wrapped around his waist and her hands gripped his shirt, and he knew.

"Oops. Sorry folks. Just looking for some air." The sound of one of the other diner's voices called them back to the world, to the chill air, to reality of life in a small town.

They jumped apart and looked as one to the doorway that was once again closed and empty. "Sorry about that, Rev. Not for the kiss but that we were interrupted. I'll never apologize for how I feel about you. Or for kissing you."

Justine touched her fingertips to her lips and shook her head, her golden hair dancing in the breeze. "I didn't ask you to. And I don't exactly know why, but I won't," she said vaguely.

He went to take her back in his arms, but she stepped to the side and slipped out of his jacket. "Maybe we'd better get back before our dinner arrives and they think we've skipped out on them. Besides, you must be freezing without your jacket."

"Not a chance," he muttered under his breath as he put his coat back on. A snowy nor'easter could blow in right then and he'd be fine and dandy.

"What?" Justine said, turning back to him.

The slight frown that creased her forehead reminded him of why they'd gone out on the deck in the first place. He had yet to learn why she'd actually sounded frightened by the idea of them dating. Once again, she'd so muddled his mind that he found himself a conversation behind.

Their dinners arrived as they got to the table and talk turned to Jon-Paul's talent as a chef. Then, as they waited for dessert the parents of one of Leslie's classmates stopped to ask Matt how Leslie was faring.

"That was nice. Them being concerned about Les," he said as he watched the couple leave and the waiter delivered a piece of chocolate cheesecake they planned to split. "But they sure don't understand eating disorders any more than either of us did at the start of this whole thing. I still can't believe some of the little insignificant things that she's brought up in counseling sessions. Things that meant little to me but gave her a lot of joy. But then, there were others just as insignificant to me that hurt her deeply."

Justine grimaced. "There's something I promised Les I'd talk to you about."

Matt was instantly stricken. "Something she didn't think she could come to me about?"

"In a way, but only because she doesn't want to hurt you. You mentioned your mother-in-law earlier. Matt, Leslie misses her grandparents terribly."

Predictably, Matt felt his jaw harden. "What they did—"

Justine put her hand over his. He hadn't even realized he'd curled it into a fist.

"Was appalling," she said in that serene way she had of calming him. "I agree. And now that we've talked about it, Leslie sees that it was, as well. But the Gainers are the girls' only link to their mother and they have been a very important part of their lives since they were born. If nothing else, they should be in on at least one or two of Leslie's sessions. Under supervision, Leslie should be allowed to talk to them about the message she got from them of falling short of Diane's perfection."

"And you want me to turn them loose on her again?"

"Matt, if I had to explain an adult perspective on them and their actions to Leslie, think how the two little ones are seeing this. Just because the Gainers hurt you, doesn't mean you should go on hurting your children by keeping loving grandparents away from them. I'm not suggesting anything but that you talk to them."

He pursed his lips. He really couldn't ignore her advice. What was that quote about removing the beam from your own eye before mentioning the speck in someone else's. "I'll consider it," he promised, then blindsided her. "Now will you consider telling me why the idea of dating me has you shaking in your shoes. I've got to tell you, it's tough on the old ego, and I did warn you how fragile the male ego is.''

Justine smiled at his teasing, but he saw that it was a sad smile.

''It isn't you, Matt. It's baggage. It's my father. And the fallout he caused in my life. I'm terrified of the same thing happening to me that happened to my mother.''

Matt felt as if she'd stabbed him. ''You don't think I'd ever—''

''No!'' She cut in, not even letting him finish his appalling thought. ''If I thought you'd simply disappear one day, I wouldn't be here. It's having a relationship with a man, any man, that terrifies me. For *my* reaction to it, not yours.''

Justine exhaled a tired sigh. Her shoulders slumped as if she were suddenly exhausted. ''To top it off, my father called again yesterday. I made an excuse why I had to hang up right away, but not before he gave me a number where I could reach him. Why I felt obligated to write it down I don't know, but I did. Now it's sitting there on my desk staring at me.''

''That's why you looked so faraway when I came into your office earlier.''

''He wants to see me. I told him I don't care why he left.''

''Yes, you do.''

That had her ears perking up and her spine stiffening. "I don't want to see him. I refuse to care about him."

"Be that as it may, his leaving changed your life. Made you who you are. You need to know why he did it."

It was easy to see the old pain well up. She blinked. "He even kissed me goodbye that morning and hugged me. I didn't know it was goodbye forever. Why should I give him a minute of my time, when he walked away and left us without a thought?"

Now he was on the hot seat. But this was too important to chicken out. "Because I'm afraid his actions are going to go on influencing your decisions and your life till you have some sort of closure. Since I very much want to be a part of that life, I have an interest in this."

It was hard to see her hurting and vulnerable—and not help. Then he got an idea. It wouldn't be easy for either of them, but whoever said anything worth having came easily.

"I'll tell you what. He's in Green Bay. And my in-laws live on the other side of the city. If you'll set up a meeting with him, I'll go with you to confront your demons. And much as I don't want a face-off with Di's parents, I'll arrange to meet them the same day. I'll come along with you for moral support, and you get to be referee when I meet with the Gainers. I'm afraid if they accuse me of causing Leslie's problems, I'm going to need one.''

Justine bit her lip and nodded her agreement just as he felt a presence next to him. Justine looked up, and Matt stood to greet Nathan and Constance.

''Constance, hello,'' Justine said.

Matt, meanwhile, shook hands with Nathan.

''Chief Trent,'' the older man said. ''We don't want to intrude but we thought we'd risk it. Do you mind if we sit? There are some things we need to discuss with both of you.

''I suppose you're wondering why I called this meeting,'' Nathan joked as he and Constance settled in the unused chairs at the table.

The joke fell a little flat. ''Actually I am,'' Matt said candidly.

''And that's why we stopped to talk to you tonight. I've been told you were trying to check out the new owner of Harbor Quay. Check no farther. You're looking at him.''

Matt glanced at Justine, who looked as surprised as he was by Nathan's announcement.

''Why all the secrecy?'' she asked before Matt could.

''Because I had very personal reasons why I wasn't ready to let others know why I was visiting Safe Harbor.''

''Come on, Nathan,'' Matt said. ''I tried to investigate the purchase. I ran smack into a call from my former boss at the Bureau. He told me to back off. For a local PD, that's called butting your head into a wall.''

''I hope it caused you no problems,'' Nathan said.

''No, but only because I backed off. My point is that it's more than personal reasons. That kind of provision is reserved for undercover operations.''

''And witness protection,'' Nathan added quietly, and nodded to Constance.

''I'd like you to meet Joseph Laughlin, my husband who I thought was lost to me six years ago.''

Justine frowned. ''But you were so upset by your attraction to him.''

Constance smiled sheepishly. ''I was. I thought I'd lost my mind when I bumped into him at the opening of Annie's B & B. He didn't look like Joseph or talk or even walk like him. Nathan was even shorter than Joseph. And Joseph had the darkest brown eyes I've ever seen. But Nathan *seemed* like Joseph—'' Constance stopped as if not sure how much to reveal. She blushed and continued. ''I realized later, he smelled like my husband.''

Matt understood. He'd recognize Justine's scent anywhere. ''Eye color's easy. Contact lenses,'' he guessed, and Nathan nodded. ''But the rest. What did you get involved in that they'd feel they had to do that much work on you?''

"About six years ago I decided to go on a missionary trip to Matto."

"Constance said the village where you were building housing had been damaged in the civil war there," Justine said. "But it was supposed to be in safe territory."

Nathan nodded. "But what the Matto government didn't yet realize was that the rebels were in league with a powerful drug lord. My team was there when mortar fire began bombarding the village, then men overran it. They killed everyone—men, women and children, including the other members of my team. I was badly injured in the first part of the assault when a concrete block wall collapsed on me. I couldn't move, but I was conscious and could see much of what went on—" His voice caught. He took a deep breath and looked down for a moment to compose himself.

It couldn't be easy to have been the only one alive after what he must have witnessed, Matt thought. Justine sniffled next to him, and he pressed a handkerchief into her hand under the table. Constance squeezed Nathan's hand.

"I woke in a government hospital in protective custody," Nathan said, holding on to Constance. "I'd already had reconstructive surgery to repair the shattered bones in my cheeks and jaw as well as both legs. They didn't know what I looked like before, so they just did their best. But the upshot of it was, I no longer had the same face nor was I exactly the same height due to the severity of the fractures in my legs.

"The Matto government as well as ours had already decided to keep my identity and survival a secret. Constance had already been informed of my probable death at the same time as the families of the other team members were informed. Both governments hoped I had seen a certain man—the drug lord, Domingo Blason."

"He was convicted earlier this year and clapped in Levinworth under maximum security," Matt said.

Nathan nodded. "He'd led the attack on the village in retaliation for taking their government's help. The Mattans had been after Blason for half a decade. He'd already killed several judges and their families. Also every DEA operative and CIA field caseworker they'd sent to gather evidence on Blason had disappeared without a trace."

"And it took this long to get him?" Matt asked.

Once again Nathan's voice broke but he gathered strength and continued. "I...was the first break in their case, but they still had to capture him before I could testify. They begged my cooperation.

"I had no real choice. To go home was to put my family in danger of his retaliation. And then there was the moral obligation I felt to all those slaughtered that day—friends and villagers alike. They said it would probably be over within a year or less. I entered witness protection and was given a new name and identity to go with the new face I'd already accidentally been given. Contact lenses completed the disguise and I was flown back to the United States as Nathan Taylor—auto accident victim in need of rehabilitation.

Nathan frowned and shook his head. "But they couldn't seem to get hold of the man, and the promised months turned into years. The break came last year. With the rebels defeated down in Matto, they had Blason on the run. His cartel collapsed with the help of the CIA, and the Matto government crack down on drug trafficking. He was captured, and even more evidence against him was found in his compound. Blason was convicted in Matto and here. The U.S. government kept him to insure that if Matto ever fell to the rebels again, he'd remain locked up."

"So now you're free to return to your old life," Justine said.

"If I wanted to. But it isn't always that easy. I had to live the life of someone else for six years. Somewhere along the line I became Nathan Taylor. While in rehab, I discovered an untapped talent. Nathan Taylor was a not-half-bad painter. Since I needed a way to support myself in a career as opposite as possible from my old career as vice-president of a global media corporation, I tried my hand at living off my artwork.

"Then my paintings started to sell better than

expected. The federal marshals were initially worried, but then we all decided I was probably safer in the public eye. Domingo Blason would never look in the pages of the *Chicago Tribune* for a man hiding in witness protection. Which was good, since the case dragged on so long.''

Nathan took Constance's other hand in his. ''That's why I was finally able to come here to see Connie. But I'd been gone over five years by then. I was kept informed of her movements, but that isn't the same. I didn't want to shock her, so I just sort of slid into town for visits, hoping to cross paths with her. She's changed quite a bit, and I wanted to get to know the person she'd become. I also needed to know she'd be able to love Nathan Taylor as she'd loved Joseph Laughlin, because we're very different people.

''Joseph Laughlin was a high-powered, workaholic, corporate executive. Nathan Taylor is a simple man who draws and paints landscapes.''

Justine leaned toward a large sketch of a lighthouse on the wall nearby. It was much like the ones hanging over the banquettes downstairs and on the walls all over The Bistro. ''*N M T*,'' she said. ''You're Nathan Mitchell Taylor. And you do more than paint pretty pictures. Your first showing in Chicago three years ago was a media event of who's who in the art-buying world.''

Nathan's cheeks colored. ''I'm embarrassed to say, people pay a great deal for my efforts. Which brings me back to Harbor Quay. I wanted to invest some of the good fortune my art has brought me in the town that has given the woman I love so much love and support. So, I purchased the Safe Harbor Apartments to spruce them up a little. I didn't want it to be common knowledge, since I wasn't sure of my future here in Safe Harbor or with Connie. I'm happy to report Connie and I will be staying on here together.''

Constance's smile broadened. ''We spoke to Reverend Burns this afternoon. He's given his permission for us to renew our vows. I guess I'll be Mrs. Nathan Taylor from now on. We decided to have a party next Saturday and explain all this to our other friends. But Nathan wanted to explain to Matt, since he nearly ran afoul of the FBI because of us. When we saw you two here together it seemed as if the Lord was sending us a message. It didn't seem fair for either of you to hear it with everyone else.''

Just then, their waiter approached with the check. They looked around. The place was empty. The four of them laughed, realizing they had accidentally closed the restaurant. Constance and Nathan said good-night then and left them alone.

Matt grinned at Justine when she turned toward him after watching the couple drift off, wrapped up in each other. She narrowed her eyes.

''You knew,'' she accused.

''Absolutely not,'' he said, digging out his wallet. ''I knew it was an FBI-protected corporation that bought the apartments, but that's all I knew. I was asked to halt my investigation and I did. And even though I was curious about Nathan, I never even tried to investigate him—he wasn't breaking any laws by being a frequent visitor.''

''Well, this will take the wind out of you-know-who's sails for a while,'' Justine said with a smile.

Matt laughed, tossed the money for the check and tip on the table and stood.

''Maybe I'll get through next Monday morning without an outraged visit,'' she said, following suit.

''That'd be nice,'' Matt said, but he wondered why the idea that the town gossip would be looking for a new target worried him. It wasn't as if he had in any way compromised Justine's spotless reputation. He'd gone out of his way to protect it, in fact.

He was worrying about nothing! He'd never do anything to harm her or her reputation. So what could go wrong?

# *Chapter Thirteen*

Justine turned to Matt to gauge his feelings as they drove away from the meeting he'd been dreading. They'd met his in-laws at a local restaurant where they'd often eaten as a family. And she thought it had gone well.

"Your in-laws seem like wonderful people," Justine said, again watching for his reaction. "I can see why you were so hurt by what they did. It must have been a shock to learn they'd offered the girls a home without your permission."

"I should have seen that they weren't adjusting."

"Will you stop being so hard on yourself. You heard what they said. They credit you with their improved mental health."

He sighed. "I guess it was a good thing that I

withdrew from their lives. That I forced them to seek their pastor's help. It must have been an eye-opener when he told them they'd been way out of line. I just wish I'd left them a forwarding address when we left for Safe Harbor so they could have let me know when they came to the place where they saw they were wrong. If they could have apologized the way they wanted to, this all would have been settled months ago.''

She smirked and shook her head. ''That faulty mind-reading problem of yours again.''

Matt chuckled and let out a tension-easing breath. ''I didn't realize how much I missed them until I saw them again. It'll be good to have them with us through the Christmas holidays.''

He let go of the wheel to take her hand and give it a squeeze. ''Thanks. I'd never have done this without your insight and support.''

''Grief does crazy things to people,'' she said, glad to have met the elderly couple and to have had some small part in reuniting a family.

''Here we are,'' Matt said minutes later. ''Admiral Flatley Park. Just let me find a place to park and we'll get to the fountain. It's to the south side of the bridge, if I remember right.''

''It's a good thing you came with me. I'd never have found this,'' she said when they arrived at the fountain. There was a damp chill in the air and the sky was gray. Justine wrapped her coat closer and shivered. She looked around, unsettled by the dismal setting and a thought that occurred to her out of the blue.

"How will I know him?"

"I have to believe he'll know you. I'd know one of my kids no matter how long it had been since I saw her."

"*You* would never not see one of those girls for one year, let alone twenty-six."

As Matt nodded, his eyes darted over her head. She turned as a tall man with heavily salt-and-peppered hair approached them. It was her father. He had the sky-blue eyes she remembered.

Matt stepped close behind her and put his hands on her shoulders the way he had on The Bistro's deck earlier in the week. She felt a little less anxious with his solid presence so close at hand.

She'd already made the decision to forgive her father, but that was because she knew she should rather than because she wanted to. He stopped about ten feet away. She saw his shoulders lift with a deep breath.

"Justine," he said, as if awed by her presence. "Look at what a fine woman my angel's become."

The use of his childhood nickname sliced through her, lancing open the wound his desertion had caused.

"No thanks to you," she said, hating the tearful quality of her voice and that she'd let the angry retort do more than echo in her head.

"No, but I tell myself every day that I did what was best."

"What was *best!*"

Matt squeezed her shoulders. "Why don't we go sit on that bench over there?" he said, probably appalled to find himself acting the part of referee rather than silent moral support.

She nodded and let him guide her, both physically and morally. This was a tired old man she'd verbally attacked. And he was her father. It was her duty to honor him even if he didn't deserve it.

Before they sat, Matt offered her father his hand. "Matthew Trent."

"Pleased to meet you."

Matt, she noticed, didn't go quite that far with good manners.

"Suppose you explain to Justine why your desertion was in her best interests," he said instead.

"Because I wasn't fit to be near an innocent child. Most of us didn't come out of the Vietnam War the same way we went in. But for some it was worse than for others. I was one of those. Have you heard of post-traumatic stress syndrome?"

They both nodded, and he continued. "Well, no one back then knew or understood what some of us were going through. Violent nightmares often translated into waking actions. Flashbacks triggered by a backfiring truck or a baby's cry sometimes turned deadly. It was different for each of us—except for the effect on those around us. Some of us were snapping, killing civilians.''

''All soldiers from Vietnam didn't do that,'' she said. Why was he going into all of this? He'd been fine. She'd waited anxiously for him to come home from work each day. He'd greet her with a smiling 'How's Daddy's angel today?' as he'd tossed her in the air. Or he'd bend over and make his arms and hands into a swing and give her and her little friends rides.

''No. Not everyone snapped,'' her father agreed. ''But it did happen. And I'd been having nightmares for a while. I had a buddy in Chicago who'd written me saying he had nightmares, too. I was able to hide it all for a while but it got harder and harder. Your mother just didn't understand. 'Just put it behind you,' she'd say. 'It's all over.'

''I went to VA doctors. They'd acknowledge that some men were having trouble. Ticking time bombs some were called. In the second World War they called it shell-shocked. Before that, other things like soldiers' heart. They said to go on with my life. But I worried I could be one of those ticking time bombs. I continued to hide it from your mother and you, but she knew about the nightmares. The doctors gave me sleeping pills.''

He shook his head as if disgusted. She couldn't blame him. So much pain because of a faraway place he hadn't been able to save, anyway. Matt handed her a handkerchief, and she realized she was crying.

"The pills worked for a while...then one night I woke to find my hands around her throat. She was terrified. Every time I tried to get near her to explain that I'd been dreaming, she would just look at me as if I were dangerous, or I'd try to touch her and she'd shrink away. She called me—" He stopped and shook his head. "No, that doesn't matter. She was a fragile woman and I frightened her.

"I grew afraid to sleep. A few days later there was a news story. It was about that buddy of mine in Chicago. He was one of those bombs that went off. He killed his wife and two kids. The whole time we were in 'Nam, he'd talked about her as if she hung the moon. I swear his stories of her got us through the worst of times."

He stopped and wiped his eyes in that way men do with the back of their wrist, like you weren't supposed to notice their tears. She pretended to do just that. She couldn't imagine his pain but she saw his shame.

But when he took a deep shuddering breath, she reached out and covered his chapped hand. He nodded his thanks and started again, turning his hand and gripping hers.

"On the news they said he'd been screaming that he'd been trying to save his platoon. That the woman and children had been wired. I'm sure he didn't understand why they were so angry. I knew right away it was a flashback to something that had happened in Danang. A woman came into camp with her two kids meaning to kill as many of our outfit as she could. He'd seen the wires on the kids and fired. He'd been hailed as a hero, though he'd never felt anything but horror over it.

"I got up the morning after hearing the news about what he'd done and left Safe Harbor. The thought of doing anything like that to you two—" His breath caught but then he forged on. "I had to keep you safe even if it meant losing you. I wandered for a while, then checked into a VA hospital in Philadelphia. They didn't know how to help, and by then my flashbacks were worse and happening while I was awake. I've been in and out of the hospital for years.

"I'm doing pretty good right now. I have a little room in a nice rooming house near a church I go to. A job that keeps me busy. I've kept tabs on you through an old friend these past few years. When I learned you were back in Safe Harbor, I just had to see you—to explain."

It seemed unreal that for the second time in less than a week a man sat recounting cruel events in a far-off land that had forever altered so many lives. And who was she to have less compassion for him than she'd felt for Nathan? Who was she to say her pain had been worse than her father's? Wasn't second-guessing the life she'd had the same as second-guessing God's grace and her gift of faith?

"Daddy," she said, and found herself enveloped in those long thin arms where she used to feel so secure—and incredibly, felt secure again. Her father had always loved her. Had never forgotten her or stopped protecting her—even from himself and his inner demons.

Matt stood on Route 7 just beyond the entrance ramp. He stared down at the flat spare he'd just mounted on the right rear of his three-year-old sedan. How it had gotten flat sitting unused in his trunk was a mystery. A deluge of freezing rain had soaked him to the skin half an hour ago. And a half hour before that, they'd dropped George Clemens off at the boarding house where Matt had insisted on driving the older man.

Just then, a tow truck pulled to the shoulder behind them, and Matt thought it was perhaps the most wonderful sight he'd ever seen. Luckily, the guy carried a tank of air and was able to fill the flattened spare. Matt counted it worth the exorbitant cost he'd be charged for air just to be able to start again for home with the heater on full blast.

It took an hour and a half to get the rest of the way home, thanks to two different fender benders that had Route 7 tied up lower on the peninsula. Justine had opted to go to Constance and Nathan's party as she was, so he could get out of his wet clothes and jump into a hot shower. He'd lingered long enough to get warm, then he'd toweled off and dressed quickly. Then they were in his cruiser—with the dry driver's seat—and on their way to the party.

They walked into the private room of The Bistro just as Nathan announced their intention to renew their vows on Christmas Eve at First Peninsula Church.

Matt mingled with the guests, but felt as if he'd been dragged backward through a keyhole for the rest of the night. He wasn't at all disappointed when Justine asked if he'd like to leave.

"I hope you aren't getting sick," she said, when he walked her to her door a while later. "You were soaked to the skin and shivering when you got back in that car." She reached up and touched his cheek with the backs of her cool fingers. He nearly sighed.

"On a scale of one to ten, that ride home came in at about a minus-fifty, but don't worry. I never get sick. It's my strong male constitution," Matt assured her. He didn't ever want to relive that ride home. He had other things on his mind now.

Justine sent him a saucy smile, and Matt felt his heart leap. All weariness fled like seeds on a spring wind and his heart soared. She was the most special woman he'd ever met. The way she'd reached out to comfort the father who'd hurt her so deeply had awed him. He stepped closer, drawn to her and her beautiful spirit.

"I'll never be able to thank you for today. But I can try," he whispered, and silently saluted her with his lips on hers. As had happened before when their lips met, the air crackled with an unexpected and unpredictable kind of electricity. His heart fluttered and stuttered and he deepened the kiss, wrapping her in his arm, unable to get close enough. She shook her head.

"Matt," she gasped when he raised his head. "Woman does not live by breath alone, but a little oxygen goes a long way." She gave a tentative smile.

"Huh?"

"Can't breathe."

Matt blinked and loosened his hold. "Sorry. You go to my head, Rev. No question about it. I'd better get out of here. Right?" he asked, half hoping she'd be weaker than he knew he should be. This was one of those times when living by a biblical code with God as the guiding force in his life was more than a little tough.

"Right. I'll see you and the girls at church," she said, her eyes still nicely glazed and her voice just a touch vague.

It was nice to see he wasn't the only one with scrambled brains. "Tomorrow's the day we're going to see Les and going to our old church since it's closer to Mittler. Remember?"

"I forgot. But then, it's been quite a day." She stood on tiptoe and kissed him quickly. "And you are quite a man. Have fun tomorrow. And give Les my love."

He wanted to ask for some of that love for himself, but told himself he'd hear the words when the time was right.

# Chapter Fourteen

Justine found herself going through the motions of a normal Sunday morning. But she doubted anything would ever look normal to her again. What did normal even look like now that Matt had turned her world on its ear?

She could still hardly think clearly. And that was not what she had expected when she unthinkingly accepted the traditional walk to her door from her date. After the kiss on The Bistro's deck earlier in the week, perhaps that had been naive, but she would never be naive again. Never scoff at the excuses women used for poor choices. Desire was perhaps the most compelling of temptations. She should know. Before Matt, she'd never have thrown caution to the wind and let a man kiss her in the moonlight. She'd never have held on for dear life while trusting him to catch her if she fell.

He'd shown a side of himself this week that she'd never have guessed at, but should have. She'd seen him as an upstanding and dedicated public servant. A loving and devoted father. A witty and chivalrous companion. And she was enormously attracted. But she hadn't seen him as the powerfully sensual male he apparently was. Then they'd stepped to her door and he'd turned her into his arms for what she'd thought was going to be a salutory kiss.

And set the air surrounding them on fire.

Justine felt her body grow warm just thinking about it. All other thoughts fled from her mind. Where she was headed? Oh, yes! She'd been on her way to the adult church from her sermon at the children's service. And for the life of her, she couldn't even remember what she'd spoken about.

Knowing she was probably red as a beet from thoughts of last night's good-night kiss, she ducked into her office to gather her thoughts. And found the phone ringing.

"Hello," she said.

"Hi. It's me. Matt. I'm afraid lunch this afternoon is out." His voice sounded a tad weak and scratchy.

"Are you hung up at the center? How is Leslie enjoying seeing the girls?"

"We didn't go. I'm sick."

That was probably an understatement, if he'd backed out on the visit Leslie was so looking forward to. If only he hadn't insisted on changing that tire to keep them from being too late.

And what about Cindy and Gina? "Are the girls home with you?"

"I got them breakfast after Cindy filled the house with smoke trying to cook eggs. Then I crawled back in bed. This has never happened before. Not since I've been alone with them."

Someone came to her door, but without glancing over, Justine held up her hand in a silent request for another moment. "Matt, do you need a doctor?"

"I don't know. I never get sick. My throat's killing me."

"Do you have a fever?"

"I can't find the thermometer."

"You are such a man. Have you eaten?"

"Oh, please," he all but groaned, "don't talk about food."

"I'm coming over there. It sounds like you have the flu."

"Then stay away. There's no sense in you getting this."

"Matthew Trent, you planted one whopper of a kiss on me last night! If I wasn't exposed then, I don't know how. You need a doctor. I'm going to check with Robert and Kyle to see which of them can see you. Then I'll be there."

Justine heard his sigh of relief and smiled. She could call Safe Harbor Family Practice from her cell phone. As she stood, she remembered there'd been someone at her doorway. No one was there now. Shrugging, she raced to her car, then called and spoke to Robert Maguire on her way to Matt's. She arranged for the doctor to meet them, and stopped at the drugstore for a thermometer.

When she got to his house, Matt was burning up with fever and couldn't even drink the tea she made him. She aired the house of the lingering smoke then piled the whole family into the car and headed to Safe Harbor Family Practice. After a quick stop at the drugstore on the way home, she got Matt ensconced in his freshly changed bed and settled the girls with a snack.

Matt obediently took his medicine and fell asleep. And after that, the afternoon seemed to fly by. There was the kitchen mess to clean. Stories to read to the girls. Lunch to make. Matt wasn't up to caring for Gina even if he and Cindy could have muddled along together alone, so Justine prepared for the next few days. Their homework had to be finished and checked and their clothes packed for a stay in her guest room.

"I don't know how to thank you," he croaked when she woke him with his five o'clock dose of medicine. Then he winced and covered his throat.

"Stop talking. I'm going to take the girls with me and drive them to school tomorrow. I arranged for Elizabeth to stop by after services while I get the girls settled at my place for the night. And I'll stop by in the morning to check on you after I drop them at school.''

''No. I'll be fine by then. I have to go to work.''

''We'll see,'' she said breezily, and kissed his fevered brow. ''I'll see you in the morning.'' She thought he was asleep before she even left the room.

Work in the morning. Right. Men were such egotists. As if the town couldn't survive without him behind his desk or in his patrol car, Justine thought as she collected the girls.

The next day and Tuesday and Wednesday morning Matt was indeed too sick to go to work or care for the girls, so they stayed with Justine. And she loved every minute of it. Neither child got sick, thank the Lord. By the time dinner rolled around Wednesday evening, Matt was up to handling their bedtime and getting them ready for school the next day. Miss Neal took them home from After-School Days, planning to cook dinner for the family while Justine made sure everything at the church was ready for the service at seven.

Just after the service Justine stopped at the ladies' room and found all the stalls occupied. So she waited.

''Did you see the way she looked when she came back in from that deck on Monday? No guessing what those two were up to out there. Not with her lips looking so thoroughly kissed," one disembodied voice in a stall said.

"If a man who looked like that had me alone, he'd have been the one who looked mussed up," a second said with a chuckle in her voice.

"I just want to know when the wedding is," the first laughed.

"It better be quick. She can't carry on that way with a father of three children and not have her reputation suffer," the third woman in the handicap stall added.

Justine couldn't help but recognize that voice. She'd had to listen to it at least once a week since her appointment in September. Geneve Peterson went on, as she was wont to do whenever she had something nasty to say. "And I hear she's been at his house at all hours these past few days. And I saw them coming out of his house last Saturday. He'd clearly just been in the shower with her in the house."

"Oh, lighten up," the first said. "She's been at his house because the man was sick, and his hair was wet because they got a flat tire coming back from Green Bay."

"And what were they doing in the city together, I'd like to know?"

Justine smothered a gasp and didn't wait to hear anything else. She just fled to her office and shut the door.

Gossip! She hated it. Her whole life she and her

mother had been the talk of the town. Growing up, she'd lost count of the times she'd walked into a store and all the adults, wearing guilty expressions, had stopped talking. She'd always known what the guilt and silence meant. They'd been talking about her mother's latest escapade. Or she would walk into a classroom amid curious stares or giggles from the girls and choking sounds from the boys.

*Sticks and stones,* her mother would tell her, and she had been right in a way back then, but this was now. She was a minister and had to live a life above reproach. There was nothing she could do to stop the talk but stop seeing Matt. Justine flinched and the room spun as an abrupt pain lanced though her. It would be like cutting her heart out.

Had it been only a few nights ago that she'd admitted to herself they were dating? How had these feelings grown so quickly? Or had that first meeting between them sown the seed that would grow into this love she felt?

How was she going to fix this?

Not that she had done anything wrong, but even the hint of scandal and her ministry and career would both be over. It was time for tough decisions. What, she asked herself, was more important? Seeing Matt? Or safeguarding her ministry?

The very fact that she hesitated to answer the question told Justine one very important thing.

Matt was taking her eyes off her ministry. Off the Lord.

Look at what she had done Sunday morning when he'd called, not even asking her help. She'd rushed off, never giving a thought to her absence in the sanctuary during services or at the social afterward. She hadn't even thought to leave a note for Reverend Burns.

Was she going to turn into her mother, after all, living her life tied to the needs and whims of a man, with no thought to the fallout elsewhere in her life?

No. Justine had worked too hard and too long to abandon her calling on the off chance that she and Matt would be able to build a life. There was no guarantee. There was even some doubt about how Leslie would react to a new woman in Matt's life. And what was worse, the girl could see it as a betrayal on Justine's part. Her pastor's part.

One thing was sure, however. If it came down to choosing between Justine or his child's mental health, Matt would choose Leslie. Which was as it should be.

The real question was, was she sacrificing God's work for a man?

"You look like a troubled young lady," Reverend Burns said, standing in her doorway. "Need a friendly ear?"

Justine looked up. When had this man not been

there for her, since she met him as a defiant teen skipping school and smoking cigarettes in the park?

"I didn't realize I was causing gossip within the church. I'm so sorry."

Thomas Burns laddered his forehead with his raised eyebrows. "Have you done anything immoral or illegal?"

"No! Of course not. I'd—"

He raised his hand. "I don't think you would, dear. And neither would anyone who knows you. As for any others, they will talk about something else next week. Now that everyone knows about Constance and Nathan, you and Matthew have simply moved to the top of the list.

"I'm not the least bit worried about any gossip or its effect on this church or its congregation because I know you'll do the right thing. What I am worried about is you—and whether you have the courage to follow the path the Lord has placed before you.

"I've seen you rushing to and fro with Matt and his children and looking very happy juggling all this responsibility. I want you to think about the advice you give the young mothers you counsel. You have to decide what is most important to you and choose it if there is a choice to be made. Soon. Before the whole Trent family gets hurt with your vacillation."

Justine nodded, feeling as if her heart would

break. Yes. The Lord had to come first. She had to break it off with Matt and follow the path she had followed for so many years before meeting Matt and his wonderful children.

Reverend Burns ambled down the hall with a little extra zip in his step. He loved Justine like the daughter he and his beloved wife had never been given. And he was sure he'd just set her on the new path God had planned for her. She would have that family she'd always so desperately craved, and maybe someday, when he retired, she and her children would be ready for her to devote more time to the other job the Lord had called her to.

One day she would make a most excellent pastor for First Peninsula Church.

# *Chapter Fifteen*

"Okay, you two monkeys, we're here," Matt said to Cindy and Gina as he pulled into the parking lot on Sunday morning. He didn't feel great but he'd made it this far.

"Yea!" they chorused, already unsnapping their seat belts.

"I can't wait to tell Reverend Clemens about the puppy Uncle Ray's giving us."

And I can't wait to just plain see her, Matt thought. Had it only been Wednesday that she'd stopped to check on him in the early afternoon? He'd missed her, but understood how backed up her work must have gotten with all the time she'd given his family. But he had thought she would stop by yesterday for at least a few minutes.

"When can we have her?" Gina asked.

Matt drew a blank. How had Gina guessed that if he had his way she'd soon have Justine for a mother? "Uh…have her?"

Cindy leaned over the seat and put her hand on his forehead. "The puppy, Daddy. You sure you're okay to come to church? Miss Neal said she'd bring us."

He kissed his daughter on the cheek. "I'm doing fine, sweetheart. Ray said by Christmas."

Gina's face appeared over his other shoulder. "So, how come you forgot about the puppy?"

He kissed her soft smooth cheek, too. "Because I was thinking of something else. Sorry, kitten. So let's get going so you can tell everyone about the puppy."

After Matt delivered the girls to their Sunday school rooms, he decided to poke his head into Justine's office. But he was doomed to disappointment. Her door was closed and locked for the first time that he could remember. What if she was sick, he wondered with alarm. She'd been near him every day for those first days that he was confined to bed.

"Kit," he called to Kit Peters, who was at the end of the hall. He thought the young woman looked more like a pixie than an art college graduate and church administrative assistant. "is, uh…Reverend Clemens sick today?"

"Sick?" Kit Peters asked. "Not that I've heard. She's here somewhere. I saw her about ten minutes ago.'' The *William Tell Overture* tinkled from her purse. ''Oops, forgot to turn my cell phone off. Do you mind if I take this?''

Matt shook his head. ''Go ahead. I need to get into the church for services, anyway.'' He turned away disappointed. He'd have to wait until afterward to talk to Justine. But after service he was once again disappointed. When he rushed down to the church hall, she wasn't there.

''She had somewhere she had to be, son,'' Reverend Burns said.

Matt turned to the pastor. ''That transparent, am I?''

''Nothing wrong with that. You starting to feel up to par?''

''Yeah. Better,'' he said absently, then heard the kids tear into the church hall.

''Reverend Burns! Did Daddy tell you about our new puppy?'' Gina shouted as she threw her arms up to the elderly man, expecting elevator service. The elderly pastor didn't flinch but scooped his daughter up as if she were a beloved grandchild.

''Reverend Clemens helped us name her.'' She prattled on about the decision to name the dog, a reddish Chesapeake Bay retriever, ''Lucy'' after Lucille Ball.

Matt couldn't help feeling just a little jealous of the time the girls had gotten to spend with Justine.

And more than that. Though he didn't know why, her absence today and since Wednesday filled him with disquiet.

Matt stared in disbelief at the answering machine and hit the rewind button. Seconds later, after slapping yet another button impatiently, Justine's voice, digitized and just a little tinny-sounding, filled the kitchen.

"Matt, I got your message about Thanksgiving dinner on Thursday. I'm so sorry but I…I can't make it. I'd made other plans. And lunch for the rest of the week is out, too. I'm really swamped. Maybe soon. Oh, and I think Lucy was a terrific idea. This will be a Christmas your girls will never forget. I'm sure Mary and Seth Gainer are going to get a real kick out of seeing the girls with Lucy. Leslie's just as excited as the little ones are about her. Well, I'd better run. Uh…bye."

Raking his fingers through his hair, Matt faced the truth. She was avoiding him. Sure, he'd forgotten Thanksgiving was this week. He was a man, for heaven's sake. Why hadn't she said something to him about the holiday? Why had she made other plans?

If she even had.

It hurt to think that way, but he hadn't seen or talked to her for six days, not since she'd stopped by his house to check on him last Wednesday. He could no longer deny what was right before his eyes.

But why?

He'd thought they were getting on famously. Had he rushed her? He didn't think so. She'd even teased him about catching his flu from his kisses. So what had changed?

"She's not coming, is she?"

Gina's question startled Matt. She had such a mournful tone that Matt felt as if a fist had squeezed his heart. He hadn't realized Gina was within earshot.

Matt shrugged, trying to convey a "not important" attitude. If she thought he saw it as no big deal, maybe Gina and Cindy would, too. "Sorry, kitten. Your old dad messed up. I forgot to invite her and now she made other plans."

"Can't you change her mind?" Cindy asked, joining Gina in the doorway to the family room from the kitchen.

"I can try, but don't count on it. She'll probably feel obligated not to disappoint her hosts."

"What's obligatered?" Gina asked.

Matt grinned. Leave it to a big word. It would distract her every time!

Matt pulled into the Harbor Quay's parking lot later that night, having asked Julie, his next door neighbor, to watch the girls as they slept. He parked where he knew Justine couldn't see his car, so she couldn't pretend to be out. She was not avoiding him for one more minute.

At first he'd told himself she was busy trying to catch up on all the work that had piled up while she was filling in during his illness. But after the phone message, he'd known it was something more.

He rang the buzzer and waited.

"Who is it?" she asked.

"It's Matt, Justine. I need to talk to you."

"I'm not—"

Matt stopped listening to her excuses and did something he'd never done before. He used his position for personal gain. He used the master key to the buildings that he had for security reasons. In less than a minute he was pounding on her door.

She yanked the door open. "Quiet. What do you think you're doing? I don't need any more gossip destroying all the goodwill I've tried to build up in this town."

"Gossip! That's why you're suddenly unavailable?"

Justine looked guiltily up and down the hall, then gestured him inside, apparently deciding that letting him in was the lesser of two evils.

"You don't know what it's like trying to live down not only my own reputation but my mother's," she said quietly as she closed the door.

He gaped at her. "You think you haven't done that and more?"

"Small-town people have long memories. I don't expect you to understand."

She saw herself through a badly distorted mirror. That was the only explanation. Her mother's she-nanigans had really done a number on her. Loving her, wanting to ease her fears, he said, "These peo-ple love you. They want you to be happy. How can you not see that?"

"Matt, I'm sorry if you were hurt about Thanks-giving, but I told Samantha Mittler I'd go there. Leslie was very glad I'd be coming."

Matt took a deep breath to try to bury the anger he'd arrived with. "This isn't about Thursday. It's about every day since last Wednesday afternoon. You kissed me goodbye and you've avoided me since. And now I guess I know why. Justine, you're letting a bitter old woman—your words, not mine—rule your life. So far, she's the only one I've come across not happy about us. The whole town was making book that we'd be married be-fore Constance and Nathan. Don't do this to us," he begged.

But Justine wasn't hearing what he needed her to. "The whole town?" she gasped, horrified, tears springing to her eyes. "You see! There can't be an 'us.' I have to let God rule my life. He was my purpose long before I met you. I'm a minister. I apparently can't be your girlfriend and do my job without causing my congregants to gossip. I won't live that way. Not again. I can't. Besides, I've come to the realization that you're taking my focus off my calling. In caring about you and the girls as much as I do, I'm not able to give a hundred percent to the church.''

Did she think he wouldn't work with her to keep family obligations from intruding on her calling? His anger swelled again. ''So you just chuck us the minute things get a little complicated and don't even give us a chance to work it out?''

''I'm sorry you've been hurt. I don't make this decision lightly, but I have to follow the calling He gave me.''

He put his own pain away and remembered the look on Cindy's and Gina's faces when they heard her message. ''Forget me,'' he said through gritted teeth. ''You had no right letting my kids love you if we meant this little to you. No right at all! I guess it's good I found out now. Fine. There is no 'us.' I guess there never was. But there's one thing I think you should think about. What if it was God who sent me into your life? What if you've mis-read His plan for your life. Maybe you've been on the same path so long you can't see all the forks you're supposed to take in the road.''

Matt, his heart breaking and his body vibrating with helpless anger, turned and left. He spent the rest of the night staring into space, trying to figure out how he was going to handle living in this small town without having the woman he loved in his life.

Justine dragged into her office while trying to keep her umbrella from dripping on the linoleum.

Rain. It was as if the skies were trying to outdo her, but she had news for the sky. It had a long way to go before it could outdo the number of tears she'd shed this past week since her face-off with Matt.

She saw Matt often but only in snatches and at a distance. She'd even heard his voice in the hall while he picked up Cindy and Gina yesterday.

Matt, she knew from Cindy and Gina, had rolled right along with his life. He'd called Mary and Seth Gainer and had taken the girls there for Thanksgiving. He'd already come and gone from the Mittler Center with them by the time Justine arrived there for dinner. Leslie had been full of excited chatter about her visit with her sisters and the plans that were being made for her to come home. Cindy and Gina had been fonts of knowledge on Sunday about what a great day she'd missed with the Gainers.

Her heart heavy, Justine opened her desk calendar to check her schedule. If she'd done the right thing, she wondered as the pages of the book blurred, why did she still feel so awful? She grabbed a tissue and dabbed at her eyes.

"Well now, if this isn't a more dismal sight than the weather," Reverend Burns said from the doorway. He walked in and sat across from her. "Want to talk about it?"

Justine swiped at her eyes again. "I'm following

the same path I have since I was eighteen. Every time before this, once I made a decision based on the Lord's will for me I felt better. Why not this time?''

''Could it be you've strayed outside His will?''

''I don't think so. I still remember the feeling of euphoria that came over me the day I realized I'd been called into the ministry. Remember? I'd been reading the tenth chapter of the Gospel of John and verse twenty-seven just spoke to me.''

'''*My sheep hear My voice,*''' Reverend Burns quoted, '''*and I know them, and they follow Me. And I give them eternal life, and they shall never perish; neither shall anyone snatch them out of My hand.*'''

''Exactly! I knew at that moment why I'd been put on this earth. I knew I was supposed to help guide His flock and be His voice, guiding others into that flock just the way you did with me. And I saw that a flock was like a family. And that God would give me a family through the ministry. I knew that one day I'd pastor a church and have a family all my own.''

Reverend Burns shook his head. ''When we spoke last about this, I hoped you'd recognized what the rest of the church and quite possibly the rest of Safe Harbor had.'' He sighed. ''Did you ever consider that the Good Lord had given you the family you so richly deserve, but in another way? A way you apparently didn't recognize? Think on that, dear. Pray on that,'' he advised.

Justine was so stunned by his words that he was gone before she even noticed.

She spent the next couple of hours in the chapel, deep in prayer. But she kept coming up with the same truths. She had wanted to feed His sheep. She had wanted to help souls as lost as she had been. But most of all, she'd wanted a family. Wanted it so badly that when given an assistant's role by Reverend Burns she'd been on the verge of bitterness. She hadn't wanted to wait any longer. She'd wanted it so badly she'd become blind to what she *could* have right now. And that was what Reverend Burns had been saying. And in her blindness she heard what she'd always heard.

Her will not His.

''What have I done, Lord?'' she whispered brokenly. But she knew. With Matt and the girls she'd had the opportunity to have a wonderful family, but, because it had looked different from the family she'd pictured, she'd thrown her chance away.

She'd rejected God's gift because she hadn't recognized its wrapping. She'd destroyed any chance for a life with Matt by committing the one trespass he'd never be able to forgive.

She'd hurt his children.

# *Chapter Sixteen*

Matt tossed his boots in the corner of the mud-room and padded toward the kitchen. Elizabeth Neal had apparently made a roast beef for dinner. The scent of it still lingered in the air some hours later. He ached in places he hadn't known he had. He glanced at his watch and couldn't believe how late it was. Or how early in the year this blizzard had hit. No one had been prepared for a snowfall like this on the fifteenth of December.

"Matt? Is that you?" Elizabeth called as the kitchen light flashed on. She saw him standing in the doorway and smiled, looking him up and down. "You look like a melting snowman. I'm so glad you're finally home. Is it as nasty out there as it looks?"

Wearily he unbuttoned his parka and hung it on

the hook just inside the mudroom. "That weather is *bad*, Elizabeth. The roads are a sheet of ice. We spent most of the night taking people home and hanging markers on their abandoned cars. I hope you prepared to stay when you brought the girls home? I know this wasn't our original agreement but…"

"Relax. Watching the girls was no problem. Herb guild canceled early on, when the forecast got so ominous. We stopped by my apartment on our way here and I packed an overnight bag. I knew it wouldn't be fit for man nor beast out there. I got the little ones all tucked in. I know you like to do that but it was getting late. Who knows if they'll call school, but I thought it best to keep them on a school schedule."

Matt nodded. "I advised the superintendent already to close, but he hasn't made the final call yet."

It was just as well Cindy and Gina were asleep, he thought. He wasn't up to being asked if he was sure Reverend Clemens got home okay. Or if he was sure her apartment house had electricity. He was ashamed to say he had an answer. He'd made sure Jake Logan had taken her home and seen Reverend Burns safely to the parsonage. And he'd hated not being able to do it himself.

"Old windbag," Elizabeth was grumbling as she bustled around the kitchen getting him dinner. He sank to the stool at the breakfast bar, frowning.

"I thought you liked Reverend Burns. In fact, I thought you two might turn out to be the next item on the Safe Harbor grapevine."

Elizabeth sent him a quelling glance. "Don't change the subject. I was talking about Superintendent Jackson. Neville's been holding school closing decisions to the last minute for years. He just likes to make everyone get up at six and listen to his brother-in-law's radio station."

Matt chuckled. It was probably the first time he'd come close to laughing in two weeks. He'd been so grouchy at the station that this morning he'd found a coffee cup fashioned like a beat-up trash can on his desk. No parent could miss *that* meaning. So Oscar the Chief of Police had apologized to everyone for being such a grouch. Unfortunately there was little he could do about the cause.

He missed Justine, plain and simple. His mind skimmed back to those magical moments they'd spent together. He'd thought for a time that life would only get better.

"So how did Tom Burns get into the conversation?" Elizabeth asked, dragging him back into the painful present. "Or do I know the answer to that? You were thinking about a certain other minister. One of the female persuasion. Want to talk about it? We all know you aren't seeing Justine any longer. I can see it isn't making either of you happy. What no one can understand is why."

"I'm not sure *I* understand, and it sure isn't my idea. Geneve Peterson must have said something to her about us seeing each other. As far as I know, no one else had a problem with us being together."

"That woman!"

"We did nothing wrong. I don't even know what Ms. Peterson found to gossip about."

"I'm sure you were careful, dear. And I'm sure there was nothing untoward going on. But we all come to relationships with baggage. Justine's is more than likely a hypersensitivity to gossip and anything that could harm her witness and therefore her ministry. Most of her young life was made very difficult by gossip. Her mother was notorious in Safe Harbor, do you know that?"

"She said there had been a lot of men in her mother's life and each one she became involved with was worse than the last."

Elizabeth nodded and sat across from him as she slid toward him a plate of delicious-looking roast beef, mashed potatoes and peas. He dug in to be polite, but food just wasn't going to satisfy his hunger for the presence of Justine.

"Her mother's behavior and her father's desertion would have been bad enough," Elizabeth said. "But one doesn't get to be infamous if gossip doesn't circulate. And adults don't often guard their tongues around their children. So she was made well aware of what was being said in the adult community by her peers every day of her life.

Day in and day out. And if that weren't bad enough, imagine Gina or Cindy walking into the post office and having all the adults who'd been talking up a storm suddenly fall into silence. You could see the awareness in her eyes. It was heartbreaking, and nearly destroyed her by time she was in her teen years.''

Matt smiled fondly. "Right. The liberty spikes.''

Elizabeth nodded. "Oh, but she was colorful. And you'd never have known how beautiful she was under the Technicolor makeup. Then Reverend Burns and the Lord entered the picture. While God heals, Matt, it is often a long and painful process. And that process may still be going on in Justine.''

"I didn't realize it had been that bad. But still. She also accused me of taking her eyes off God's work. I never, for one moment, expected her to change or abandon her ministry. That's one of the things I love about her. Why would I want to change that? I appreciated her help while I was sick but I didn't ask for it. I've been raising the girls alone for two years. I'd have managed.''

"I'm sure you would, dear.''

"Then, what?''

"Hmm. Well, now. I don't quite get it myself. I've seen her with the girls. I have no doubt she loves them and I would think she'd want to be a mother to them. She was absolutely wonderful juggling everything while you were sick. And she looked like she was having the time of her life doing it. No. I don't know what all that stuff she told you meant. And I'm sorry. You all seemed to be such a perfect fit.''

Matt nodded and ate because he had to, not because Elizabeth's perfect meal didn't taste like cardboard. He'd thought they were perfect together, too. A match made in heaven. But he'd used every argument he had and it hadn't changed her mind. His hands were tied.

And his heart felt as if it were starving.

''That tree, Daddy,'' Leslie said. Matt picked up the Christmas tree and eyed it carefully. The shape was all wrong. Though big, it wasn't the caliber of tree he was used to. He looked around the lot while still holding the one the girls were considering. But by the twentieth of December the lot was pretty picked over. He'd put this trip to the church's tree lot off until Les got home today because tree day had been his and the girls' domain since each of them got out of diapers.

''Turn it to your left,'' Les said.

''Your other left, Daddy,'' Cindy shouted, and giggled.

In spite of the joy he felt at having Leslie home and doing so well, he was dreading this holiday. Les had taught him a thing or two about handing control over to God in the past weeks. But he was still struggling to understand why things had gone so wrong between him and Justine. Now he'd be facing questions from Les as soon as she learned how far his relationship had gone with Justine and how far it had deteriorated. Since their breakup was still news, he knew she was sure to hear all about it.

"Reverend Clemens, hi," he heard Les say, and his stomach dipped.

"Welcome home to Safe Harbor," Justine replied.

"Thanks. We stopped here on our way from Green Bay. I'm so excited about Lucy. I finally get to see her. We're bringing her home today."

"It sounds as if your family will be complete for Christmas. We all missed you at After-School Days. Will you be back after school starts up again?" Justine asked.

Matt wondered how he could detect her scent on the brisk wind with all the pine smell wafting through the lot. And he wondered how long the sound of her—and the sight of her—would make him feel as if a hand were squeezing his heart. Seeing her at church on Sunday was bad enough. He just couldn't go on picking them up, knowing she was in the building, avoiding him.

"If Miss Neal isn't free after school," he practically growled from behind the ugly tree, "I'll hire a sitter. That is, unless Les wants the job."

"Oh. Well, I guess I'll see all of you at church from now on. I'll, uh…miss you," Justine said.

And he was suddenly very glad the tree was so full at the top. That way he hadn't seen the hurt look that must have gone with the tone in her voice.

"Yeah," Cindy said, sounding confused. "We'll see you at church still."

"I guess I'd...better buy my tree and get home to decorate it," Justine said, and picked up the sorriest excuse of a tree Matt had ever seen and dragged it off.

"Daddy, are you okay back there?" Leslie asked.

"You're not sick again or nothin', are you?" Gina asked. "Daddy was real sick when you were in the hostible," she went on. "And Rev took care of us."

"Gina, you're not supposed to call her Rev even if Daddy did," Cindy admonished. "Right, Daddy?"

"Let's just pick out the best tree on the lot and get it home before someone else takes it," he said in as cheerful a tone as he could muster. "I'm not sure this is it." He knew having this particular tree in his house would ruin what was left of his Christmas spirit. It would remind him that he wasn't behaving very well and that he'd been unable to make himself travel the high road.

Les came to his rescue. "How about that one?"

Matt dropped the offensive tree and made a grab for the next choice.

* * *

Leslie watched as her father tied the tree on the roof of the car. He was acting really weird. Christmas, always his favorite season, seemed to have her dad really bummed this year. Even finding the best tree they'd ever had hadn't lifted his spirits. And he'd practically growled at Reverend Clemens, the nicest person Leslie had ever met. And what was that about Daddy calling her Rev?

"Okay, Cindy, what's up with Daddy and Reverend Clemens?"

Cindy shrugged. "We spent a lot of time together when you were at the clinic. One night he even took her out all by herself. Like a date. And they went to Green Bay together one day when Daddy made up with Nanna and Grandpa. Then Daddy got sick and we went and stayed with her. We had such a good time. But after that we hardly ever saw her. And Daddy got, well, not grouchy— sort of sad all the time."

"And he teased her and called her Rev. They were dating and now they're fighting. That's got to be it!"

Gina leaned against the corner of the building and crossed her arms. "She was supposed to be my mommy. Now she's not. It's not fair. I had it all figgered out!"

"You didn't say anything, did you?" Cindy demanded.

"You told me not to. See where that got us. A sad daddy and still no new mommy."

Leslie stooped down and huddled Cindy and Gina in a tight circle. "It isn't over yet. Did you see how sad they both were? Here's what we're going to do. First I'm going to talk to Miss Neal at church tomorrow. And Cindy, see if you can get Mrs. Laughlin to help."

"Help with what?" Cindy asked.

"Matchmaking."

"But isn't that the thing Daddy said I can't do?" Gina asked.

Leslie grinned and gave Gina's chin a gentle little pinch. "Exactly. And you aren't going to do or say a thing. That way you can't get in trouble." *Or mess this up,* she added silently to Cindy with a speaking look. "But Daddy never told Cindy or me not to try it. And he can't tell adults not to. So keep it on the Down Low. Okay?"

Gina nodded solemnly. "Down Low? Oh! Quiet. Right!"

"Hey, what's up with you guys?" the subject of their conspiracy asked. "Planning a Christmas present for dear old Daddy?"

Leslie turned. "Yes. Actually. And you'd better love it because we already do!"

# *Chapter Seventeen*

Justine checked her reflection. The red velvet dress she traditionally wore on Christmas Eve wasn't cheering her at all. She should have just stuck to basic black. At least that would have suited her mood, she decided and stalked away.

On her way to the coat closet she stopped at the sad excuse for a Christmas tree in her living room. "We're a pretty sad pair, Sparky." She fingered one of its dry branches. "Spangles and ribbons a holiday spirit do not make, huh?"

She sighed and checked her watch. It couldn't be put off any longer. It was time to get to the church. If only she hadn't agreed to be Constance's maid of honor. If only she'd asked who Nathan had invited to be his witness before she'd agreed. What had possessed the two of them to force her and Matt to stand so near one another at a wedding ceremony?

It was just plain mean of them!

The drive to the church unfortunately took only five minutes, and the regular service, filled with poinsettias and carols, took just an hour. Then it was time.

On the way to the altar, Justine didn't feel at all like a participant in a joyous event. She felt more like a prisoner walking those last steps to her execution. Or like a martyr on the way to the arena to meet the lions. She would have to stand next to Matt. See indifference in his beautiful, obsidian eyes.

She and Constance stopped at the altar just as Nathan and Matt arrived through the side door. The happy couple was all smiles as they joined hands before Reverend Burns. She and Matt, however, both wore identical neutral expressions. At least on her part, that look of neutrality was difficult to maintain. As she gazed across at the handsome man she loved so deeply, all she wanted to do was cry. If only she hadn't made such an unforgivable mistake.

It didn't seem possible that he'd become such a part of her life so quickly. The only explanation was that Matt had indeed been sent by God and she'd unforgivably scorned His beautiful gift of love. She prayed she would never make that mistake again.

But in the meantime, she couldn't live this way. She just couldn't. She might be all cried out, but the pain of seeing his warm dark-chocolate eyes look at her as if she were a stranger was more than she could bear. It was time to move on and find a new safe harbor where her wounds could heal and she could get on with her life and her ministry. She was certainly no good to herself or anyone else the way she was.

Justine started when Constance thrust her bouquet into her hands so she and Nathan could exchange rings. After the final pledge with the exchange, the organist struck up the traditional recession for a wedding. It only then occurred to Justine that she'd have to take Matt's arm and follow the Taylors to the back of the church. Her eyes met Matt's and he turned away, walking off in the other direction, leaving her standing there as he joined the family she'd rejected in her blindness and stupidity.

To cover the awkward moment she shrugged and took her traditional seat to the left of the podium. Reverend Burns walked to the microphone and with a nod of his head signaled the organist to move from "The Wedding March" into a joyous rendition of "Deck the Halls." His booming voice roused the congregants into the lively song that ended the service.

There were two celebrations that night. One in the church hall and a small intimate one for Constance and Nathan at the Lighthouse B & B. Justine had promised to attend both, so she went downstairs to the church hall and circulated among the congregation.

She decided to stay longer than she'd planned at the church's Christmas celebration so, hopefully, Matt would be gone from the little party Annie and Russ Mitchard had decided to throw for Constance and Nathan.

"What on earth are you still doing here?" Reverend Burns demanded as he walked up to Justine and an elderly woman she'd been counseling about her need to enter a managed care facility. "I'm sure Mrs. Weber will excuse you," he continued, and took Mrs. Weber's hand, smiling fondly at the elderly woman. "Justine was supposed to have left quite a while ago for Constance and Nathan's reception."

"Goodness, dear. You were the maid of honor. What are you doing wasting your time with a silly old woman like me when you have a celebration to attend?"

Justine shot an annoyed look—the first she could ever remember—at Reverend Burns. "You are not a waste of my time, Mrs. Weber. I like spending time with you. And I still will, even if you decide to move into Rest Harbor."

"And I appreciate that, but right now you shoo."

"Yes, Justine. Shoo," Reverend Burns said a bit

smugly. "And while you're shooing you can give me a lift up there."

*At least that way I'll be sure you get there*, the old pastor thought.

Leslie looked out the parlor window of the Lighthouse B & B. Everyone was there. Everything was in place. Except that it was getting late and Reverend Clemens still hadn't shown up.

"What if she doesn't come before Daddy decides it's time for us to leave?" Cindy fretted.

"Girls, it's fine," Miss Neal said as she rushed up to them. She sat next to Leslie on the settee under the parlor window and took a deep breath. "I called Thomas…uh…Reverend Burns, I mean. We were concerned Justine might just go home after the way your father left her standing on the altar. So the reverend decided to make sure she came by getting her to bring him. They should be here any minute."

"Okay, but what about the quilt?" Leslie asked.

"It's on the deck. On a bench where they're sure to see it. The Women's League made it for them, and we're bound and determined to make sure they use it!"

"Cindy, you know what you have to do?" Leslie said, checking again.

"Gina and I have Daddy."

"And I handle Reverend Clemens," Leslie confirmed.

"And don't forget that she has to know you approve of her and your father," Miss Neal reminded her. "Constance says Justine was worried that you'd be against your father marrying again."

"Why would she think that? Mom practically ordered him to. I've had it all planned for weeks," Leslie said. "They played right into my hands. At least, until they broke up! Why'd they have to complicate everything?"

"Who's to say why what happens between people happens?"

"Well, it doesn't matter now 'cause I'm going to fix it."

"Child, you're wearing the most devious smirk I've ever seen," Miss Neal said, and Leslie took it as the compliment Miss Neal's smile said it was.

"They're here," Cindy whispered. "Oh, I hope this works. Oh, what if I do it wrong?"

"Leslie, you stay here. Cindy, Gina, come with me. We'll go upstairs and rehearse one last time," Miss Neal ordered, and took each of her sisters by the hand.

Reverend Burns and Reverend Clemens came in a few minutes later on a gust of cold wind, and Leslie began to doubt the plan. Until she saw her dad walk into the hall and spot Reverend Clemens. And then she relaxed. He wasn't mad at her at all. He looked like someone had punched him. Almost like he was going to cry. Then he backed away while looking at Reverend Clemens—till he bumped into Mrs. Maguire and almost knocked her over.

At first Leslie thought her father looked so sad that Reverend Clemens must have brought a date, but a quick glance at their pretty minister quashed that theory. All she was doing was helping Reverend Burns out of his coat and taking off her own.

Hmm. It looked like her daddy had it bad. Maybe this *would* work. After all, Leslie grinned, if they didn't want to freeze they'd have to share the quilt. Mrs. Constance was right about that. And if they were huddled that close they'd have to talk. Leslie had a feeling that if they did, it would be a happy Christmas, after all.

Matt rounded the corner after nearly knocking Wendy Maguire off her feet and went to gather up the girls. He had to get out of there. He'd been uncomfortable enough after making an idiot of himself at church. Why he'd never thought of the recessional he didn't know, but he hadn't. He'd thought they'd all just go back to their seats.

Then Nathan had turned and taken Constance's arm. And the couple, the only buffer between him and the woman he so desperately loved, had stepped into the aisle and left him staring at her. He hadn't known what to do. But he'd known what he wanted to do. He'd wanted to kiss her there before God and a good portion of the town and demand she reconsider. Instead he'd panicked and torn his gaze from hers, retreating to his pew with the girls. Not until he'd gotten to his seat and seen the look on all three daughters' faces had he realized that his actions had looked cruel.

Maybe he could just go home and kick their Christmas puppy and complete his transformation into the Safe Harbor Scrooge.

"Daddy."

Matt looked around for Gina, whose voice sounded small and muffled. "Kitten, where are you?"

"We're here, Daddy," Cindy said, her voice oddly halting.

Matt lifted the tablecloth that trailed to the floor. "What are you two doing under there?"

"We was hidin' from Leslie." Gina said.

"But now I think we made her mad," Cindy said. "She didn't come to find us."

Matt dropped to one knee and continued to peer into the recesses of the gate-legged table. "Why do you think that?"

"'Cause now *we* can't find *her*. We looked just everywhere," Gina told him in that serious, no-nonsense way she had about her.

Cindy brightened. "Not everywhere! We didn't look upstairs. Maybe we should look there and, Daddy, you should look down here."

"Good idea, sweetheart. We have to be going now, so you two run on upstairs."

Matt stood and, as the girls scrambled out, noticed that everyone else had gravitated to other rooms. Then Nathan walked in from the kitchen as Cindy and Gina rushed toward the stairs.

"Matt, is it okay for Leslie to be out on the deck at this time of night by herself?" he asked.

"Is that where she is? Thanks, and if I don't get to see you before I leave, congratulations."

He and Nathan shook hands, and he headed for the deck doors. He stepped out, closing the cold air outside with him. But when he turned and looked around, there was no one on the deck. He walked to the rail, wondering if there were steps Les might have gone down, but once he got there he realized they'd be steps to nowhere. The deck overlooked the rocky bluff below. And there was no other egress to the deck but the door from the dining room he'd just come through. Where could Les have gone?

Leslie kept Reverend Clemens in sight. When Mrs. Mitchard gave her the high sign she knew it was show time.

She rushed up to Justine. Time was everything in this! "Reverend Clemens, can you help me? I can't find the kids. Dad asked me to keep an eye on them. I think they don't want to leave so they're hiding from me."

"It isn't that big a house." Reverend Clemens said. "This won't take long."

Leslie smiled in relief. ''You start in the parlor. I'll start upstairs. Thanks.''

As Leslie walked off toward the stairs she heard Reverend Clemens ask Mrs. Maguire if she'd seen them. And the reverend went into the dinning room.

The deck doors opened just as Matt turned to go back inside. His heart stopped beating and he watched in breathless surprise as Justine stepped out. She turned then and gasped when she caught sight of him. Whirling, she grasped the doorknob and twisted it. Or tried to.

Just then, Les appeared, then Cindy, then Gina, and they unfolded a huge poster. It said, *Merry Christmas, Daddy and Rev.*

''Don't you dare, young lady!'' Matt shouted as he rushed to the doors. But before he got there, the draperies swished closed to a chorus of giggles.

Justine, still holding the doorknob, dropped her forehead on the door stile and groaned.

# Chapter Eighteen

"I apologize," Matt said stiffly. "They just don't understand. I should have seen this coming. Except, this is so unlike Les."

"This seems to be where I came in." She shivered. "But it was quite a bit warmer that first Sunday in September."

Matt remembered seeing a quilt on one of the benches, so he went to snatch it up. The little scamps had certainly prepared well for this trick.

The doors rattled as Justine shook them in desperation. Then she started pounding. "Come on, you guys," she yelled. "This isn't one bit funny!"

He tried to tell himself she was only this desperate because it was so cold out there, but after the shameful way he'd been behaving he knew how untrue that was.

"Here," he said, handing her the quilt. "I really am sorry about this. I promise to deal with it and give all three of them a good talking-to."

She wrapped herself in the huge quilt, still not looking at him. "I'm afraid you'll be lecturing half the town in that case. Reverend Burns included. This took an incredible amount of timing and involved quite a conspiracy. I imagine everyone in there has to be in on it. Otherwise, someone would have heard me and let us in by now."

She had a definite point. Was he to find no peace in this town? Once again his anger built. He turned away from the forlorn figure she made, huddled near the door wrapped in the huge quilt. "I can't live this way," he snapped. "I can't handle being thrown together with you like this. It's bad enough I have to run into you by accident and see you around town."

"Don't worry, Matt, I intend to tender my resignation as soon as I can find an appointment to another church. With the shortage of ministers being what it is, I shouldn't need to stay here much longer. Don't be so angry with them. Please. They didn't understand. They were only trying to help. Which is why I think you'd better share this with me. I have a feeling we aren't getting inside anytime soon."

Matt saw little choice. The brisk wind cut through his suit, chilling him to the bone, and he didn't need to be sick for Christmas. Apparently the kids were already in for a huge disappointment tomorrow, considering they thought he was about to bring them Justine for a mother.

He looked around for a spot that had a little windbreak. There was a sheltered nook near the house with a bench that would have to do. "Okay. I guess I don't have much choice. Let's sit over there, out of the wind."

Justine nodded and followed, fumbling with the quilt and trying to keep it from dragging. She was almost there when she dropped a corner and tripped over it. He lunged forward and caught her before she could tumble to the deck.

Justine looked up, her eyes wide. The light from low-voltage lanterns lining the deck glistened in her beautiful eyes. Then he realized the glistening was tears.

"Come on," he said gently, taking the quilt and holding it so she could sit with it draped behind and under her. Then, careful not to touch her, he sat and tried to get warm. But a shiver worked its way up his spine, broadcasting the truth of his discomfort.

Justine closed her eyes when Matt shivered. And she prayed.

*Lord, if this is You using our friends and the children to bring us together, I know You'll give me the words. Maybe I don't have to leave Safe Harbor. Maybe You've given me a second chance.*

"Maybe you should put your arm behind me," she suggested. "If you got closer, we could get the quilt to overlap a little in the front. We'd be much warmer."

Looking like a man sentenced to a slow death, Matt dropped his arm behind her shoulders, then inched closer. Justine scooted even closer, hoping to weaken his resolve, and soon they were hip to hip. With a silent sigh, she sank into the enveloping warmth and shelter of his arms and the warmth the Wedding Ring quilt let them share.

The Women's League had been working on this Wedding Ring quilt at meetings for the past couple of months, and she'd stitched part of it herself, thinking it would wind up being for Constance. Now she wanted it for herself. And Matt.

They sat in silence for a few minutes, and she knew it was her responsibility to break that silence. After all, her foolishness had created the gulf between them.

"I'm truly sorry, Matt," she said, looking straight ahead. She didn't think she could handle that indifferent expression she'd seen in his eyes earlier in church. "I really never meant to hurt you. Or the girls. *They* seem to have forgiven me, at least."

"Kids are resilient, but since it seems to mean so much to you, you're forgiven. Now you can leave Safe Harbor with a clear conscience."

He sounded so self-contained. What if he was

back to trying to control everything? What if she'd done damage to his walk with the Lord? Hurting him spiritually would be so much worse than losing him.

"Please don't judge God by one of His servants," she begged, choosing her words carefully. "We're just flawed beings, hoping to be His light in a murky world. Unfortunately, we make mistakes. Sometimes they're big ones."

"I never had any problem with you in your capacity as a minister. It's on a personal level that I was angry with you. Don't worry that I'm blaming God for the way you refused to fight for us."

"I was wrong not to. You can't know how much I regret the things I said and did and even thought."

Matt stiffened. "Are you saying you've changed your mind? That you think you could ignore the gossip?"

Justine darted a desperate look his way. "Are you saying you'd be willing to give me another chance to ignore it?"

"I want to," Matt said. His arm tightened, and she felt his lips against her hair. "You can't know how much I want to."

Once again tears sprang to her eyes. "But…"

"But I do have the girls to worry about. They love you and I have to be sure *you're* sure. I can't let this hurt them again."

Justine nodded. "So where do we go from here?"

"I talked to Elizabeth about your reaction to the gossip. She told me what life was like for you growing up here. I didn't realize your mother's private life haunted you in public. I think I understand why the gossip upset you so much. And I think if that was all there had been to it, we could have gone on with hardly a ripple. I think you could and would fight for the right to have a man in your life without Geneve Peterson and people of her ilk implying that you've done something wrong. But it was more. I need to understand what." He tilted her chin upward so their gazes locked. "Justine, I love you. I love you for who and what you are. I never meant for you to think I wanted you to change a single thing about you. For me or for my daughters. And I certainly don't want you to give up your ministry. I just wanted to make you happy and be happy with you."

Again she nodded her understanding. "It was about family, Matt."

He frowned. "You don't want a family?"

"I want a family more than anything on this earth. I've always thought God had called me to the ministry with the express purpose of rewarding me here on earth with a safe family."

"A safe family?"

"A *church* family. I was afraid to consider having a real one because a husband could desert me the way my father did. But in my drive to get the position that would give me the family I thought God meant for me, I forgot why I wanted the position in the first place. Somewhere along the line I started to think only about the position.''

''That's why you were so upset about not being given the assistant pastor title. Without that title, you were less sure to move into the head pastor role when Reverend Burns retires.''

She nodded and put her hand on his chest over his oh-so-kind heart. The steady beat somehow reassured her that this time she had not misread God's signals. This was a second chance. But they were talking about the rest of their lives, and she needed to know he understood where she'd been coming from.

''Don't forget I had just been passed over by the search committee at my Chicago church. But now I see their unfairness sent me here. *God* sent me here. To meet you. I trusted you the way I never thought I could and I fell in love with you. And I loved your children. But I was so blinded by the past that I couldn't see beyond it to the future. The right future. The future God had laid out for me all along. And so I rejected the gift He sent the same way the world rejected His son. I didn't recognize the family He sent the way His Chosen People didn't recognize Him because the package wasn't what I'd been expecting.''

''So you understand that I could have handled

being sick and caring for Cindy and Gina if I had to.''

She reached up and combed her fingers through his tousled hair. ''You didn't need me anywhere near as much as I need to be with you and take care of you. Reverend Burns made me see that I'd made the right choice that day I left the church to go to your place. It was the right choice for me. And you. And the girls. Someday the job of head pastor will open up at First Peninsula and I may be ready for it to be my right choice then. But it isn't right for me now.''

''What is?'' Matt whispered against her lips, his voice husky and low. It played along her spine, teased her nerve endings.

''I want to be your wife, Matt. And be a mother to your wonderful, adorable children. And maybe you could be the father of a couple of our children, too?''

He grinned. ''So we'd be what? Mr. and Reverend Trent? Reverend and Mr.? How's that work, anyhow?''

Justine chuckled. ''Well, now, I'm not sure, but I'm sure we can figure something out.''

Matt lowered his head and covered her lips with his. In the background the church bells rang the midnight hour.

''Merry Christmas, darling,'' he whispered against her lips. ''I think this is the best Christmas gift the girls ever got for me.'' He kissed her again thoroughly and they lost track of time until a muffled cheer penetrated their euphoria. They jumped apart and looked as one toward the locked doors. The curtains to the dining room now stood open. Grouped in front of the doors, applauding and cheering, were Leslie, Cindy, Gina, Reverend Burns and Elizabeth. To one side of them were Russ and Annie Mitchard with their adopted son, Drew, and Holly and Alex Wilkins and their twins. To the other side stood Kyle Hart and Gracie Hart, and Constance and Nathan and their two daughters along with their son-in-law.

A lot of happiness had come to Safe Harbor and to the congregation of First Peninsula Church in the past year. Justine was suddenly sure a great deal more would follow in the days and years ahead.

In fact, she was counting on it!

\* \* \* \* \*

Dear Reader,

I hope you've enjoyed *Home to Safe Harbor* and all the other Safe Harbor books. When my editor asked if I was interested in joining the other wonderful authors slated to create Safe Harbor and the townsfolk, I jumped at the chance and the challenge.

The added challenge of writing about a female in ministry certainly got my creative juices flowing, and I picked my theme of giving control of our lives over to God. Within hours I knew Justine would struggle with her role in the church and the difficulty many women in ministry still face. Then I mixed in an inner struggle with her most worldly desires and how they could fit with God's plan for her just to make things interesting!

Matthew came next. I decided he'd lost much in his lifetime but had many blessings, as well. I gave him a protector's personality and a challenge in the form of a problem with one of his precious daughters. Parenthood is our most important and difficult responsibility in life. Our most rewarding, too. And Matt, being a hero, had to be a good father who was loathe to share his responsibility or the control of their lives or his to anyone—even God.

It didn't take long to know what silent specter could be shadowing one of his children undetected. Twice, anorexia has touched a child close to my family and twice, full of fear for their children, parents ventured forth seeking an answer and help. And as Matt and Justine learned, this is an insidious disease that manifests itself with symptoms that lead to one conclusion—dieting as the cause—while the problem is something more complex and difficult to solve.

I would like to thank the Renfrew Center and its staff, whose invaluable help aided not only me in the writing of this book but a very special girl in her time of need. I urge anyone who sees the signs described in *Home to Safe Harbor* in any young person to visit www.renfrew.org or e-mail questions to inquiries@renfrew.org. Then find help.

Philadelphia is blessed with the Renfrew Center on whose facility, principles and treatment plan I based the Mittler Center. Only, the personal story of the Mittler family was fiction. And above all, don't forget to pray for your loved one to the Great Healer for whom no disease is too much.

Love,

*Kate Welsh*

# FINDING HOPE

### BY
## BRENDA
## COULTER

Dr. Charles Hartman didn't need anyone—or so he thought. But after crashing into his life, college student Hope Evans had taken on an unlikely mission: to bring out the "nice guy" in Charles and put him on the road to faith. Suddenly the usually strong-willed M.D. was having the hardest time saying no!

**Don't miss**

## FINDING HOPE
**On sale July 2003**

*Available at your favorite retail outlet.*

Visit us at www.steeplehill.com

LIFHBC

# Love Inspired®

# THE CARPENTER'S WIFE

BY

# LENORA WORTH

No one wanted roots more than Rock Dempsey.
He finally met the woman he wanted to share his life
with in Ana Hanson. But nothing had ever come easy
for the woman he hoped to have and to hold forever.
Would it take some divine guidance from above
before she would become the carpenter's wife?

**Don't miss**
# THE
# CARPENTER'S
# WIFE
**On sale June 2003**

*Available at your
favorite retail outlet.*

# An Accidental Hero

BY

# Loree Lough

Book #1 in the *Accidental Blessings* miniseries

A head-on collision with burned-out rodeo star Reid Alexander is the last thing Cammi Carlisle needs! Pregnant, widowed and alone, Cammi is returning to her family's Texas ranch in search of forgiveness. Little does she know that the kind, chivalrous man who just might be the answer to her prayers is seeking *her* forgiveness....

## Don't miss

# AN ACCIDENTAL HERO

### On sale July 2003

*Available at your favorite retail outlet.*

Visit us at www.steeplehill.com

LIAAH